W9-CFV-620

STILL THUGGIN'

MEL G

STILL THUGGIN'

MEL G

Copyright © 2016 Mel G

All rights reserved.

ISBN: 1536846406
ISBN-13: 978-1536846409

STILL THUGGIN'

MEL G

STILL THUGGIN'

Chapter 1

Trae was able to catch Sky's falling body right before she hit the ground. He passed his piece to Ty so that he could use both hands to carry her. They needed to be getting out of there right away. Before Trae could take one step, the triplets had their guns trained back on him, which caused everyone else to follow suit.

"I hope you don't think you're going anywhere with her," Julio barked.

"Are you motherfuckers serious right now?" Trae asked. "Fuck that shit you're talking about. I'm about to get her out of here. Either follow or y'all can stay y'all asses right there."

With that, he turned and rushed from the house, completely disregarding the guns aimed at him. He knew that his crew had his back, so he wasn't worried. His only focus was on making sure that Sky was okay.

Stacey had already instructed his men to put their guns down and disperse. Stacey and the triplets left out and followed behind Trae.

"Yo," Stacey called out stopping Trae. "You ride with me. We already have a doctor on standby waiting for us to get there."

At that point Trae didn't care who was driving, as long as they were taking them in the direction that would lead to Sky getting some help, he was okay with it. Trae gently placed Sky in the back of the truck and climbed in behind her. The entire ride, Stacey sat staring at Trae through the rearview mirror. Trae tried to ignore him, but it had begun to piss him off.

He was glad when they finally made it to their destination and he was able to get away from this nigga. In the past, he had never had any issues with Ace. Trae wasn't so sure about that now. He wasn't even sure where he and Sky stood right now. It was obvious that she seemed to think that maybe Trae had a hand in everything that had transpired, but he honestly didn't have a clue who she really was. Yeah, he was aware that Ace had a sister, but barely anyone who worked with them even knew her name, let alone what she looked like.

Trae carried Sky into the house and followed Stacey as he led the way to the doctor.

"You can leave now," Stacey told him after Sky was situated on the bed.

"Look, man. I'm not going any damn where, so don't even waste your time," Trae told him. Trae knew what Stacey and the triplets were capable of, but he wasn't about to back down from any man.

"Well, actually I need for the both of you gentlemen to step out for a moment," Doctor Baranov informed them.

Stacey was about to object but thought against it. He needed to talk to Trae alone so they could get a few things cleared up. Stacey headed to the door and opened it for Trae to leave out first. Trae looked back to the doctor and Sky before he reluctantly left out of the room.

"Let me holler at you for a second," Stacey requested. Trae's eyebrow raised slightly as he gave him an odd look. "I'm not on no sketchy shit, a'ight? But there are some things that really needs to be discussed."

Trae nodded his head and followed Stacey away from the room that Sky was in and down the hall to an office. Stacey closed the door behind them and motioned for Trae to take a seat.

"What's this about?" Trae asked after they both were seated.

"What's going on with you and my sister?" Stacey asked, getting straight to the point. "How did you even find her?"

"Before I answer any damn thing, I want to know how the hell your ass is alive and where have you been this whole time?" Trae questioned. "What the fuck happened?"

"What happened was that Santana's punk ass took my fucking father out, thinking he was going to be running shit. Obviously, it ain't work out that way and shit was gravy until I wanted to bring Sky in next to me."

"But why would you even want to involve her?" Trae cut in and questioned. "Sky's not cut out for no shit like this."

"I don't know what Sky you're referring to because she's as thorough as they come. It's in her blood," Stacey told him. "Pops was planning on retiring soon before everything went down, and we had been grooming Sky for years. Hell, she probably could even give you a run for your money."

"Ain't no way we're talking about the same Skylar, man." Trae ran his hands down his face in disbelief at what he was hearing.

He didn't want to believe it, but he couldn't argue with facts. Even Noc had been trying to tell him. After their little impromptu training session, Noc had called Trae praising Sky's skills. Noc even told Trae that he thought he should do a little more investigating and figure out what was really going on with her. Shit was just too suspect.

Sky tried to downplay everything, but Noc knew that there was more to her story. Trae never got the chance to confront her about everything Noc said because by the time he had returned, Sky had been kidnapped.

"Believe it," Stacey told him. "But we gon' have to finish this discussion later. Siah's calling."

Chapter 2

"What the hell's going on?" Stacey barked as he entered the living room where everyone else was.

Jonas and Julio were not feeling Trae's boys being in their space. They respected Stacey's authority, but they felt as though he had made the wrong decision by trusting them. They weren't too fond of outsiders and Trae and his people weren't looking too favorable right now.

"Man, tell these niggas to calm all that extra shit down," Bo spoke. "The only reason we ain't wreckin' shit right now is out of respect for Trae and Sky."

Noc stood off in the background waiting for someone to make the wrong move. He planned on being cool right now, but at the end of the day, his goal was to protect his brothers at all costs.

"All of y'all be easy," Stacey told them.

"Ace, my nigga, I respect you and everything," Mills started. "But I don't take orders from you. Until those motherfuckers kill it with all that hostility, won't shit be easy."

"Chill," Trae finally spoke. "We good here. Right, Ace?"

Stacey shared a look between the triplets before they all backed down. "Right," Stacey confirmed.

Jonas raised his hands in surrender. "If they're good, then I'm good."

"Whatever," Julio said. He backed down out of respect for Stacey, but he wouldn't let his guard down around them.

"Mr. Santiago," Doctor Baranov called from behind them. Stacey and the triplets all rushed to him. "Oh, my apologies. I meant Mr. Stacey."

"Doctor B, you know you have to be specific around here," Julio told him. "How is she?"

"She's better," the doctor informed them. "She's asking for her brother."

Stacey looked around to everyone, before blowing out a nervous breath and following behind the doctor. Before they made it to the room, Doctor Baranov stopped and turned to Stacey.

"Before we go in, I want you to know that her body is under a lot of stress and her blood pressure is extremely high. She's not really cooperating right now," he informed him. "I told her that it's not good, considering her current condition and that she should at least try to get some rest."

"I'll try to talk some sense into her," Stacey told him.

"Good luck with that, son," the doctor said patting him on the back. "You're definitely going to need it."

When Doctor Baranov opened the door, Stacey was greeted by an angry Sky. The doctor left back out of the room, leaving Stacey and Sky alone. Silence filled the room as they both stared at each other. Neither of them spoke a word. Sky couldn't believe that she was actually sitting here looking at her brother. She thought that she had just awakened from some horrible dream, but he was here in the flesh.

Sky left out a piercing cry as her emotions finally got the best of her. Stacey rushed to her side to comfort her. Sky was scared for him to even touch her. For the past three years, Sky believed her brother to be dead. She still had nightmares about the night of his supposed death.

"How is this possible? I watched them kill you right in front of me! They killed you, Stacey!" She cried in his arms. "Why would you do this? How could you leave me out here alone?"

"Sshhh, baby girl," Stacey soothed her. "I'm here now and that's all that matters. You know I would never leave you, Skylar."

"But that's... That's what you did!" She sobbed uncontrollably. "You left me! I needed you!"

"Sky Baby, you have to understand that I thought you were dead, too," Stacey tried explaining.

"I don't understand, Stace." She sniffled. "What happened?"

"Look, first you need to calm down before we have this talk," Stacey told her. "Doctor B told me you've been in here cutting up and what condition is he talking about?"

Sky looked away from him. She was scared to tell him of the news she had learned a couple days ago. True, she wasn't a kid anymore, but Stacey had a way of bringing that out of her. Sky never wanted to feel like she'd let her brother down in any way.

"Sky," Stacey said turning her face towards him. "Whatever it is, you can tell me."

She took a deep breath and looked into her brother's eyes. His gaze was cautious, and she could tell that he was anxious to know what was going on with her.

"I'm pregnant," she said while dropping her head.

"Nah, don't do that, Skylar," Stacey told her. "What you holding your head down for, like you're ashamed or something?"

"Are you mad?" she asked.

"Why would I be mad, Skylar? As much as I hate it, you're a grown woman now and I know a lot has changed since we've been apart." Stacey pulled her tighter into his arms while getting comfortable on the bed.

"I'm assuming that it's Trae's," Stacey inquired. Sky nodded her head as more tears began to fall from her eyes. "What's the problem, baby girl? He wants you to get rid of it or something?"

Stacey had already started to hop from the bed, but Sky caught him by the arm. "No, Stace! That's not it," she hurriedly said trying to calm him. "He doesn't know. I just found out myself and the first time I see him, we're facing off in a damn showdown."

Stacey relaxed a little and resumed his position on the bed. "Do you plan on telling him?" Stacey asked.

"I really don't know," Sky said. "With everything that's been going on, I don't even know if I can still trust him. He knew you were my brother this whole time. On top of that, he's been working with Santana."

"Sky, listen to me." Stacey turned to look at her. "Trae and his people have had ties to our family for years, way before Pops was even killed. Both of our pops were really close to each other back in the day, which is why Trae was even working with Santana in the first place."

"I don't care, Stace," Sky cut in. "Do you expect me to really believe that he didn't know who I was? I'm not buying it."

"Sky, seriously?" Stacey asked. "Look, there ain't too many people that I would even vouch for, but Trae's a good dude. He's a loyal dude. Why do you think they ended up at the warehouse tonight?"

"Because he fucking works for Santana," Sky argued.

"Sky cut out all that stubborn bullshit out and listen to what the hell I'm telling you," Stacey told her. "Who do you think sent them where y'all were?"

"Wait, how did you even know about me and Trae?" Sky asked confused.

"I didn't, but it wasn't too hard to put two and two together," Stacey answered. "That nigga had put a whole damn APB out on your lil' ass. Would've thought you were the president's daughter or something."

Sky laughed at her brother. She missed moments like this between them. "Whatever, Stacey." She laughed.

"But for real though," Stacey said becoming serious. "If those niggas can go that hard for you, then they're okay with me."

There was a knock at the door before Julio stuck his head in the room. "How you doing, Sky Boogie?" Julio asked.

"I'm better now that I have my Bubby with me," Sky said, squeezing Stacey.

"After all this time, you still call me that shit." Stacey laughed.

"So," she told him. "You always gon' be my Bubby. But don't think that mean I'm not still mad at you. You too, Ju-Ju."

"Damn, what I do?" Julio asked.

"Why didn't y'all tell me?" she asked.

"Don't even be mad at them. I asked them not to say anything," Stacey informed her. "I didn't want anyone to know I was back."

"I'm not just anyone, Stace! You're talking like you just went away on vacation or something," Sky fussed. "You faked your own damn death!"

"I ain't fake shit." Stacey frowned. "Those motherfuckers thought they killed me and I let them continue to think that. I was wearing a vest but I still got hit seven fucking times."

He pulled away from her so he could show her a few of his scars. He had been hit twice in his side, twice in his neck and jaw, and three times in his legs. The bullet in his neck had come so close to his spine that the doctors weren't even sure if they were going to be able to move it without causing even more damage. One of the bullets had even shattered his left femur.

For the first six months, Stacey had been in a coma after going into shock during surgery. After the doctor was able to stabilize him, Josiah had him airlifted to Columbia so that he would be safe. When he finally awoke from the coma, he learned that Sky had been killed during the invasion and Santana had held a memorial service for them both.

Stacey was broken after hearing that news and felt as though he had failed Sky. The only thing that motivated him during his rehabilitation process was his thirst for revenge and wanting to avenge his sister's death. It took him almost a year of therapy to get him back to his old self and it didn't take long for him to start seeking answers. With the triplets' help, he was able to stay in the loop of what was going on in Miami during his absence.

Now he wished that he had focused on getting at Jayceon instead of Santana, and maybe he would have found out about Sky sooner. Sky told him blow by blow what happened with her since the night of the invasion. Jayceon must have been praying really hard to whoever he prayed to, because even though death was inevitable for him, he really didn't want Stacey to have gotten ahold to him. They definitely did him a favor by killing him the night they saved Sky.

"So, umm. What we gon' do about our little house guests?" Julio spoke.

"Oh, damn," Stacey said. "I forgot all about them. I'm sure Trae's going to lose his mind if he doesn't see for himself that you're okay. You want me to get him for you?"

"I guess you can," Sky answered hesitantly. "Could you guys not mention anything about the baby?"

"Gotcha, baby girl," Stacey assured her before motioning for Julio to leave out of the room with him.

Chapter 3

Sky was a nervous wreck as she sat waiting on Stacey to send Trae to her. Just a few hours ago they both had been facing off, ready to blow each other's heads off. Even though she felt a little better after her conversation with Stacey, Sky wasn't sure how Trae was feeling right now. He had made it clear a thousand times how big he was on loyalty and trust. She was sure that she wasn't looking too trustworthy and loyal to them right about now.

There was a light knock at the door and she already knew it was Trae on the other side. She tried to shake off her nerves and prepared to face him. After she let him know that it was okay for him to enter, she held her breath and waited.

Trae walked in and closed the door behind him. He leaned against the door with his hands in both pockets as he stared at her. Trae didn't attempt to get close to her. They would probably only end up arguing if he was to speak, so he chose to get his thoughts together. Even though he was still pissed at her right now, he needed to see with his own eyes that she was okay. Regardless of how he was feeling, that didn't outweigh the love he had for her.

"Do you plan on just standing there?" Sky asked, finally breaking the silence.

Trae still didn't speak. He continued to stare at her with his emotions blank. Sky couldn't really tell what was going through his mind right now. His unwavering stare had her feeling very uneasy and she began to fidget with her hands.

"Trae, if you don't plan on talking to me then why are you here?" she asked with irritation evident in her voice.

The fact that he continued to ignore her pissed her off even more. If that was his goal, then he had surely enough accomplished that. Without warning, Sky threw the glass pitcher that had been sitting on the nightstand table, causing it to shatter a few feet from where he stood.

"Fucking say something!" She yelled.

In the blink of an eye, Trae had made it to her bedside and grabbed her up by her shoulders. "Don't you ever in your life try no shit like that again," Trae spoke calmly before releasing her from his grasp, causing her to fall back against the bed.

The way he was handling her had Sky in her feelings. She hopped back up and attempted to swing at him, but he was too fast for her and caught her wrist midair. He pinned her arms behind her and brought her roughly against his chest.

The door to the bedroom came flying open and Stacey, along with the triplets, Mills and Ty, had all rushed to see what the commotion was about. When the triplets saw that Trae had Sky pinned, they instantly drew their guns, which caused the same reaction from Mills and Ty.

"Raise your hand at me again and see what happens," Trae snarled. "I don't give a damn about them being in this room, Skylar. If I don't raise my hands to you, don't think you gon' get away with doing that shit."

"Trae," Stacey firmly called out. Trae glared at Sky for a few more seconds before releasing her.

"Give us a minute, please," Trae requested with his eyes still on Sky.

"Hell no," Julio spoke up.

"Let's go, Ju," Stacey said heading to exit the room. Before he left out, he stopped and turned back to Trae. "Don't be stupid, nigga."

Trae waited until everyone exited the room before he addressed Sky. She had begun to cry, but her tears meant nothing to him right now.

"Just leave Trae," she yelled at him.

"Why the hell are you mad?" Trae yelled back. "I'm the one that deserves to be mad, Skylar! Don't ever in your life try no shit like that again!"

He began to pace the floor in an attempt to reel in his anger. Sky really had him wanting to strangle her right now. This is not how he pictured things to be when they were finally reunited.

"How could you keep all of this shit away from me, Skylar?" Trae asked in a calmer tone. "We've been together for seven fucking

21

months and you didn't think that this part of your life was something that you should have shared with me?"

"Because it was my past, Trae," she tried to argue. "A past that I wanted to forget."

"How the hell is that your past when it's the whole fucking reason we're here right now?" Trae yelled.

"No, we're here because you got me caught up in your shit! I was doing fine before I got with you," she yelled back.

Trae stopped and stared at her. "Oh, you were doing fine before me, huh? So, were you doing fine when your own fucking best friend and so-called boyfriend were plotting on your ass for a fucking come up? Wait, so were you doing fine when that nigga almost killed your simple ass and they left you for dead? Were you doing fine then, Skylar?"

"Don't sit there and try to put this shit on me, because we both know the truth. Yeah, being with me might have put you in a little more danger, but don't sit there and make it seem like I'm the sole reason them niggas were after you," Trae argued. "I'm the one that's been out here busting my ass and risking my fucking life and freedom for your ungrateful ass. And for what? You ain't even have the decency to keep it gulley with a nigga and tell me what the fuck was up from the jump! So if anybody should be mad, it's me!"

"Fuck you, Trae!" She stood up and screamed. "I didn't ask you to do any of that shit! You chose to!"

"Because I love your stupid ass," he yelled in her face. "My dumb ass was willing to do whatever the fuck it took to make sure that you were okay! I don't need you to ask me to do a damn thing, because as your man I'm supposed to do that shit with no hesitation! Period!"

Everyone, but Stacey, was still standing on the other side of the door listening to the entire argument. They were all shaking their heads at the two of them.

"Man, they ain't never went at it like this," Ty said shaking his head. "I don't even think they ever even had a righteous argument before."

"Like real shit," Mills started. "Those two motherfuckers in there need some counseling."

"And all of y'all nosey motherfuckers need to go find y'all some business," Stacey spoke from behind them. "Let them get that shit out. They good."

They all laughed and walked away from the door. At least the argument between Sky and Trae had the group distracted long enough to where they weren't pulling guns on each other every other second.

Stacey opened the door and stepped halfway inside. "Look, if this conversation can't be had without all this damn yelling, then y'all may need to wait to talk," Stacey told them. "Skylar, the doctor just sat here and told you that your blood pressure is high as shit and you need to be taking it easy."

Sky huffed and folded her arms across her chest. She didn't know what had gotten into her. Even though things looked pretty suspect, Sky knew that Trae wasn't a snake. Over and over again he had proven his love and loyalty to her and never gave her a reason to doubt him or his motives. Even with all of that, she still wanted to rip his head clean off his sexy ass body.

If she was is denial about her being pregnant before, she surely wasn't now. Now that she knew, she had started to take notice to how much of an unstable crybaby she had turned into. She was not looking forward to this pregnancy if this is what she was going to be like. With the way she was acting, she would be lucky if she even made it through this pregnancy without Trae killing her.

Trae took a seat in the chair that sat across from her bed and dropped his head in his hands. Stacey shook his head at Skylar and motioned for her to talk to Trae. She rolled her eyes at him, causing him to give her a firm glare. No matter how long they had been away from each other, Sky still knew not to play with Stacey. She reluctantly sat down at the edge of the bed and faced Trae. Stacey left back out of the room, locking the door behind him.

"Listen, Trae," Sky started. "I honestly wasn't trying to be deceitful by not telling you about this part of my life. But I mean, how was I supposed to?"

"What do you mean how? There have been plenty of opportunities and you just shut down on me every time."

"A part of me still couldn't bring myself to trust you completely. I mean look at everything I've dealt with," Sky said. "I've known Jay and Draya practically my whole life and even they turned on me for a dollar."

"Are you serious?" Trae asked with a raised brow. "Skylar this entire time I've been sitting here breaking bread with a man who wants my woman dead and you don't think that's something I would like to know? And fuck that nigga and her. Hell, that ain't really even the reason why this shit is bothering me so much."

He scooted closer to Skylar and took her hands in his. "Do you realize how close you've gotten to my family? Baby girl, your whole reason for being in Atlanta was because you had a price on your head. You don't think that's something that you should have shared with us? You put us all in danger and we were blind to the shit."

Sky knew that he was right and understood where he was coming from. She had acted selfishly and didn't consider the possibility of them being brought into the crossfire.

"I'm sorry, Trae," she apologized. "You guys have nothing to do with all of the drama that's surrounding me. I would never forgive myself if something were to happen to your family because of me."

"Sky, you don't get it." Trae shook his head. "You've become a part of this family. It's not just me out here, ma. We've all been out here fighting and didn't even know why we were fighting, but none of that mattered because we were doing it for *you*. And for you to really sit there and question my motives and not trust me?"

"I'm sorry," she whispered with her head hung low.

Trae placed his finger under her chin and lifter her head until her eyes met his. "Stop with that sorry shit, ma," he told her. "I don't want to have to go through this same thing with you again, Skylar. There's too much at stake for us to be keeping secrets. If you can't be honest and keep it real with me going forward, then we need to end this right now."

The look on his face let her know that he was serious. She couldn't bear the thought of not being with Trae. Tears began to form in her eyes with just the thought of Trae walking out of her life.

"No more secrets, Trae," she declared.

He pulled her into his arms and held her close. Sky silently cried on his shoulder as she contemplated telling him about the baby. She knew that she had just promised him that there would be no more secrets between them, but this was one she just wasn't ready to share yet. She still hadn't made up her mind if she wanted to keep the baby or not.

They never really talked about having kids and she wasn't really sure if Trae even wanted children. Hell, she couldn't even tell you if she wanted kids. For now, she was going to keep this to herself and pray that it didn't come back to bite her in the ass.

****

Sky sat up talking with Trae for the remainder of the night. They were finally able to talk without getting the other too riled up. Even though she didn't want to, she told him about everything that had happened during the time she had been kidnapped. It was a bit more difficult for her to discuss the rape with Trae because she didn't want him to look at her differently. Regardless of if she had been with Jayceon in the past or not, he still had no business violating her the way he did.

Trae was visibly upset as Sky cried while she tried to finish. He couldn't take seeing the pain that it had caused her. He was pissed that he hadn't gotten to Jayceon first, but even more pissed because he felt as though he had failed Sky.

He removed her arms from around him and stood with his back to her. He couldn't bear to look at her right now, which made Sky nervous. She wasn't sure if he would want to still be with her after what had happened. Another man had touched what was his, and now she was damaged goods.

"Trae, I'm sorry," Sky cried out just above a whisper. "I know that you probably don't want—"

He turned in her direction so fast that it startled Sky and caused her to stop midsentence. She could see the anger in his eyes and didn't know what to say next.

"Don't even think to finish that sentence, Skylar," Trae told her in a serious tone. "What that sick motherfucker did to you was not your fault and I don't want you ever thinking that I feel differently about you because of that. Do you understand me?"

She lowered her head, feeling like a child being scolded. "Yes, Trae."

Trae walked back over to her and pulled her back into his arms, before lowering his lips to hers. "I love you, Skylar. Nothing's going to change that."

"I love you, too, Trae," she told him as she snuggled into his neck and inhaled his scent.

"I'm going to go run you a bath, okay?"

Sky watched as he got up and headed into the adjoining bathroom to draw her bath. She laid back on the bed and listened as he got everything situated for her. A few minutes later, he came and swooped her into his arms and carried her into the bathroom. He stood her on her feet and began to carefully remove her clothes. Every time a new bruise or scar was revealed to him his jaw would clench and she could see the vein throbbing in his temple.

"Trae," she said drawing his attention to her face. She reached down and began to stroke his head, which was her way of calming him. "I'm fine, baby."

He nodded but didn't speak. After he removed her last piece of clothing, he led her over to the tub and helped her in.

"Are you going to get in with me?" she asked after he took a seat on the edge of the tub.

"Baby, I don't want you to feel like we have—" She waved her hand to cut him off.

"Trae, I've been through hell these past weeks and I just want to be in your arms," she told him. "I need that right now, baby. Hold me, Trae."

No more words were spoken as he stripped out of his clothes and joined her in the tub. After everything that she had shared with him, he was very cautious and unsure of her current mindset. He didn't want her to feel like she needed to rush herself to be intimate with him, but Trae quickly realized that that wasn't the case. She didn't need him close to her for sexual reasons. She wanted to feel safe again and being is his arms gave her that sense of security she so desperately needed.

Chapter 4

"Look, I already know that more than likely Trae ain't going anywhere," Stacey started. "Which I'm going to assume that means that neither are y'all."

"You right," Bo spoke up. "Not with these trigger-happy motherfuckers here. They'll probably shoot his ass first chance they get."

"I know good and well you ain't calling nobody trigger happy, nigga," Mills laughed.

"Shut up, bitch. Don't act like you ain't just body a nigga granny the other day," Bo retorted.

The tension between both crews had died down a little. They all still had their guards up but as long as Stacey and Trae were cool, then they would be too. Stacey and the triplets were currently occupying one of the properties that his father left behind. No one knew of the estate and Stacey was glad because he knew that his so-called "godfather" wouldn't have hesitated to snatch it up in he and Skylar's absence.

STILL THUGGIN'

Stacey ushered everyone to the bar and billiards room since it seemed like they were about to be stuck in each other's presence for a while. Besides, they had more important things to worry about that may require them all to put their differences to the side.

"I heard some crazy ass stories about you three motherfuckers." Bo pointed to the triplets and laughed as they all poured them up a drink from the bar. "No lie. I thought we did some ruthless shit, but y'all might take the cake."

"Don't believe everything you hear, *mi amigo*," Jonas spoke. "Could be lies."

"Nah, I highly doubt that," Ty joined.

"What can I say?" Josiah shrugged. "We're no angels. Far from it actually."

"So, I'm guessing ain't nobody going to address the big ass elephant in the room," Noc finally spoke for the first time, not in the mood for stories. "You've been alive this whole time, Ace?"

"Long story," Stacey said keeping it short.

"We ain't got nothing but time. We at least need some type of understanding on what the hell is going on around here. Whether we like or not, we in this shit now," Ty said.

They all sat around and listened while Stacey gave them a rundown of what was going on. To say they were shocked would be an understatement. Even with the information that they had gotten from Draya, they still weren't prepared for everything Stacey laid on them.

"Y'all sure are pretty comfortable up in here," Sky said catching their attention.

Stacey quickly moved to her. "What you doing out of bed, Skylar? You're supposed to be resting." Stacey scolded her.

"I know Stace. I just wanted to see everyone," Sky said pouting.

"Sky Boogie," Mills called out to her as he opened his arms to embrace her.

"What you just called her?" Julio barked.

"Chill, Ju-Ju," Sky warned.

"What's up with this dude? We were just chillin'," Mills said shaking his head. "Nigga wishy-washy as fuck."

"Julio's been calling me Sky Boogie since we were kids," Sky explained. "He doesn't like anybody else to call me that."

"His ass been territorial over Sky since she was born. You would think his ass was her brother instead of me," Stacey told them. "Don't pay him any attention."

"Whatever." Julio huffed.

"How you feeling, sis?" Noc asked as he pulled her into his side and kissed her forehead.

"A lot better now that I'm back with all of my men. Can't dwell on everything else right now," she answered. "Where are my girls?"

"They'll be home soon. Had to send them away for a minute so we could handle business," Ty informed her.

"Yeah, or else Trish was probably going to kill Trae's ass." Bo laughed.

"Oh my Jesus," Sky shrieked. "What happened?"

"She blacked when everything first went down and tried to beat his ass," Bo told her. "You know that girl don't play about you."

"Should have seen how bad her and Taz did yo' girl Draya." Noc chuckled.

"Wait, what? When did all this happen?" Sky asked, confused.

"When we were tearing the damn city up looking for you," Trae answered.

"Where's Draya now?"

"She's no longer an issue," Noc answered.

"Seriously, I really appreciate all that you guys have done for me," Sky said becoming emotional. "You didn't have to, but y'all took me in when I had no one and treated me like family."

"Baby, how many times do I have to tell you that you are a part of this family?" Trae wiped the tears from the corners of her eyes.

"Suck that shit up. Don't tell me you've turned into a big ass crybaby since I've been gone," Stacey teased her. "Damn, I've got to toughen you back up."

"Whatever." Sky rolled her eyes. "I'm going to lie down. How long will it take for y'all to get the ladies here? They are coming here, right?"

"I've already set everything up. They should be here tomorrow afternoon," Ty told her.

"Hold on. I'm not too sure on them coming here with all this other shit going on. How many people know of this spot?" Trae questioned Stacey.

"Y'all are good here," Stacey answered, already knowing what his concern was. "Your family will be well protected and there's more than enough room."

"We running a bed and breakfast now?" Julio mumbled. Jonas laughed and elbowed his brother.

"Get some rest. There's a lot of shit that we need to discuss, but that can wait until tomorrow," Stacey told them all.

****

"Where is she?" Sky heard.

"Skylar!"

"How y'all just gon' come up in somebody else shit with all that damn yelling?" she heard Ty fuss.

Sky dropped what she was doing in the kitchen and rushed to the foyer. The ear-piercing shrieks that came from the women could probably be heard throughout the entire manor. Tears fell from Trish's eyes as she pulled her friend into a tight embrace.

"Sky," Trish cried in a whisper. "I thought you were gone. I don't know what I would hav—"

"It's okay, T. I'm here and that's all that matters." Sky cried.

"So, Sky's the only one y'all big headed asses see?" Trae called from behind the group.

"Stop hating, Trae. Let us have this moment," Taz said wiping her eyes.

"I got someone I want y'all to meet," Sky told them.

She led them to the kitchen where she had been before they arrived. Stacey was still seated at the island eating from the platter of food that Sky and the chef had been working on.

"Bubby." Sky whined. "I told your greedy behind to wait. Foolin' with you, everything gon' be gone before it's even time to eat."

"Man, I'm a grown ass man with a grown ass man's appetite. I need to eat and you taking forever." Stacey laughed. "Chill, Sky Baby. I won't eat anymore."

"Damn," Kay said under her breath. "Do y'all see how fine this nigga is? Who the hell is that?"

Sky grabbed Stacey's hand and walked him over to where the ladies stood. Trish looked down at their hands joined together, then back up at Sky. There needed to be some explaining going on and quick. Trae was just in the other room and Trish knew that her brother wouldn't hesitate to act a fool if something funny was going on.

"Umm, who's this, Sky?" Laiah asked curiously.

"Ladies, this is my brother Stacey. Stacey, these beautiful women here are Laiah, Trish, Taz, and Kay," Sky said introducing them all.

Sky watched as their eyes grew big. She could tell that they were all shocked. As far as they all knew, Sky only had one brother and he was dead, so for him to be standing in front of them, they all needed a moment to soak it all in.

"What type of lifetime bullshit do y'all got going on around here?" Kay asked dramatically. "Y'all just taking me on all types of rollercoaster rides. I need a damn drink."

"I'll bet money that she's with that cat, Bo," Stacey whispered in Sky's ear, causing her to burst out laughing.

Trish heard him and laughed as well. "You're right on the money. Those two fools are one in the same," Trish told him.

"Hell, I'm with Kay on this one," Taz said. "Y'all couldn't give me a million dollars to believe this shit is normal. This straight movie action. Y'all could make some money off this. Get a reality show or something and name it *Mafia Mami* or some shit like that."

"Mafia?" Sky questioned while laughing. "Who's in the damn mafia, Taz?"

"Yo' lil ass. Don't try to front now," Taz said. Sky couldn't do anything but laugh.

"Sky Boogie, are y'all finish with the food yet?" Julio asked as he entered the kitchen. He stopped when he saw that they had even more company. "Oh, I'm sorry. Didn't know that your guests had already arrived."

"You're fine, Ju-Ju and everything is almost ready," Sky informed him. "Ju, these are my girls Trish, Taz, Laiah, and Kay. Y'all this is my cousin Julio."

"It's nice to meet you," Trish spoke up after she snapped herself from the daze he had her in.

After he greeted them, he tapped Stacey and motioned for him to follow him. "It was nice meeting you ladies. Make yourselves comfortable," Stacey told them. "Sky Baby, let us know when everything's ready."

The ladies were mesmerized as they watched the men walk away. All Sky could do was shake her head at them and laugh. These heifers were acting like they had never seen good looking men before, which Sky knew was far from the truth because they got to be around some every day.

"I'm going to need for y'all to stick y'all tongues back in and close your mouths," Sky joked.

"Damn, I think I'm in love," Trish gushed. "Julio is sexy as fuck."

"Nuh uh. Don't even think about it, T. They ass just got to the point where they aren't pulling guns out on each other every two seconds. So whatever you're thinking, drop it," Sky warned.

"You can have my brother, but I can't get your cousin? Damn, that's messed up Sky. At least I ain't trying to get Stacey, even though he can definitely get it, too," Trish joked.

"Man, what. That nigga can have every single one of my babies," Kay said, high-fiving Trish. "Girl I'll be like, 'Bo who?'"

"Go over there and grab a bottle of water with y'all thirsty asses." Laiah laughed at them. "Just met these damn men and y'all ready to bust it open. I'm telling Bo and Mills."

"Fuck them," Trish and Kay said in unison.

"Talk that shit now." Taz laughed. "Ain't nobody got time to be going to war over y'all thot ass."

"I swear," Sky agreed. "Come help me take this stuff outside. We're eating out back."

Sky and the chef had prepared what looked like an entire feast for lunch. They had everything from seafood platters to barbeque. At first, she thought she may have went overboard with the food until she thought about just how much her brother and cousins could eat, and not to mention Trae and the rest of the crew. If it was one thing that they could agree on, it was their love for food.

The ladies each grabbed one of the platters of food that was placed on the islands and followed behind Sky as she led them to the back patio. When Stacey noticed them carrying the food out, he rushed to assist them.

"Didn't I tell your hardheaded behind to tell me when everything was ready? We could have come and got all of this," he scolded.

"Well it's out here now, Stace," Sky said letting him take her tray.

"Oh, my lord and sweet baby Jesus," Kay said as she suddenly stopped walking. Almost causing Laiah to bump into her.

"Dang, Kay. You can't just be stopping in front of people like that," Laiah fussed. "What the hell you looking like that for, crazy?"

Kay ignored Laiah and turned her attention to Sky. "Bitch, why the hell didn't you tell us that it was three of them?" Kay asked in a hushed tone.

Trish finally took notice to what Kay was referring to and noticed Julio standing alongside two other men who were the spitting image of him. Sky shook her head at them, before waving her cousins over.

"Josiah and Jonas, this is Trae and Ty's sister Trish, their cousin Taz, and that's Laiah and Kay," Sky introduced. "Okay, now that everybody knows everybody we can finally eat."

"Fucking triplets," Kay whispered the Trish. "Man, I have to have one and then they fine as hell. Lawd please forgive me for all these unholy thoughts that's running through my mind right now."

"Chill. Bo's looking dead at you," Taz whispered as she passed her to sit her tray down.

"Come here, Kayla," Bo called out to her. The look on his face and the fact the he used her whole name let her know that he had peeped how she was eyeing the triplets.

"Oooh, you in trouble now," Laiah taunted. "That's what yo' fast ass gets."

"Forget you, Lay. Ain't nobody scared of Bo's ass," Kay said as she left them and headed over to Bo.

They had finished setting the food out and it was finally time to eat. After everyone got settled at the table with their plates, Stacey stood to bless the food. When he concluded his prayer, Trish looked up to find Mills staring a hole through her.

Trish knew he was going to feel some type of way about her not speaking to him when they arrived. It also didn't help that she chose to sit next to Julio instead of him. She hoped that he didn't think that just because they had sex before the ladies were sent off that everything between them was okay.

Lunch was going perfect and everyone seemed to be getting along. They were all conversing and joking like they had known each other for years. Well, everyone except for Mills. He was too busy trying to see what was so damn funny that it had Trish cheesing all is Julio's face.

"What's so funny, T? I want to laugh, too," Mills said interrupting them.

"None of your business. We were having a private conversation," Trish snapped at him.

"Seems kind of rude to be having a private conversation at a table full of people," Mills said becoming more aggravated.

"What we have going on over here is really none of your concern?" Julio spoke with a smug look on his face.

"I don't think I was talking to you, playboy," Mills said mugging him.

"Whoa, what's with the animosity?" Julio chuckled. "Why so serious?"

Julio was taunting Mills and everyone at the table knew it. For some reason, those two seemed to constantly butt heads. Sky knew how her cousin could get and she also knew how Mills could be. Instead of letting this pissing contest continue, Sky chose to intervene.

"Ju," Sky spoke in a warning tone. He got the message of threw his hands up in surrender. "Can we at least make it through lunch before the guns come out?" She may have said it in a joking manner, but she was still very serious.

"And we definitely don't need that," Trae spoke. "Ain't that right, T?"

The way Trae was glaring at her told her everything that he wasn't saying in front of everyone else. He wasn't happy with how she and Julio seemed to be a little too cozy with each other and he was sending her a warning. Trish chose to take heed to that warning because she didn't need things to hit the fan because of her. Trae may have seemed cool right now, but it was certain things that could make all that coolness go out the window. She was one of them.

Trish was mad that Mills had tried to put her on the spot in front of everybody, but she would deal with him later. The only reason he even said something was because he knew that one of her brothers would follow-up and put a stop to whatever it was going on.

This was nothing new. He was always trying to cock block and Trae and Ty didn't think anything of it because they were all that way with all the ladies. Mills motives were different now. He was no longer just trying to look out for someone he saw as his little sister. He saw her as his woman now and he wasn't about to let any nigga try to step on his toes. If Trish thought that he was about to sit here and play these games with her, then she was sadly mistaken. It was time for them to get an understanding. And quick.

Chapter 5

After lunch everyone had pretty much went their separate ways so that everyone could get settled. Laiah and Kay were both obviously rooming with their men, so that only left Trish and Taz. Stacey offered each of them their own room since the estate was so massive, but they chose to just room together instead. They were already in an unfamiliar environment and Taz wasn't trying to be alone. She could have easily stayed with one of the twins like she always did, but she wanted to spend time with Sky and everyone else.

Trish wanted to room with Taz for different reasons though. She knew that Mills would be trying to make his way to her room the first chance he got and hoped that by Taz being there it would possibly buy her some more time.

Luck obviously wasn't on her side. The moment she heard the knock at their door, she knew that it was more than likely him. Taz shook her head and laughed, while making her way over to open the door. Mills walked in the room and headed straight for her.

"Preston, I am not about to deal with you right now, so you might as well—" He quickly reached for her, causing her to shut up.

Instead of responding to her, he snatched her up by her arm and ushered her towards the adjoining bathroom. Mills closed the door and stood staring at her without saying a word. Trish rolled her eyes and folded her arms across her chest. She refused to let him think that he had her intimidated, even if it was the truth.

"You really trying to test my patience, man." He paced the floor in front of her. "You must want me to act a fuckin' fool. Is that it?"

"Preston, I don't give a damn what you do. You ain't my problem or business," Trish said smartly.

"What's your problem now? We were just good before y'all left."

"Nah, nigga. The sex was good, not us," Trish told him. "I'm not like them ditzy ass broads that you're used to dealing with. You can't just expect sex to fix every damn thing."

"What the fuck, man?" Mills released a frustrated breath. "Ain't nobody trying to use sex to solve anything. We talked about this shit, Trish. I was fucking with her before we even started foolin' around heavy."

"That doesn't matter. That bitch should never feel like she could even approach me in the first place," Trish fussed. "How does she even know about us messing around to begin with?"

Mills looked away from her and began to rub the back of his neck. He didn't want to tell her that Porsha had found out about them after she went through his phone. He had slipped up and ended up falling asleep at her place. He may not have slept with her, but she did end up giving him head.

It wasn't his intentions to let things go that far with her. The only reason that he had went over to Porsha's in the first place was because she kept blowing his phone up complaining about sharp pains in her abdomen and swore up and down that she couldn't get in touch with anyone else. Even though he knew there was a big chance that the baby wasn't his, there was still a possibility that it was, and he wasn't about to let anything happen to it.

"Oh, so you silent know, huh?" Trish asked, snapping him out of his thoughts.

"T, you really blowing this shit way out of proportion right now," Mills told her. "Look man, I went over there to take her to the doctor a while back and the bitch went through my phone. That's it. I don't know why she's coming at you, because me and that hoe weren't even together to begin with. I smashed a few times and kept it moving. Then, she wants to pop up talking about she's pregnant with my seed."

"You don't have to explain anything to me, Preston. It ain't like we together." Trish shrugged. "I really don't care."

"We not together?" Mills' nostrils flared. "Quit playing with me, Trish."

"See, that's your problem. You always think somebody playing. I'm dead ass serious." Trish was ready for the conversation to be over with.

Mills moved from where he was standing and stood in Trish's face. "Let's be clear on something. I'm a grown ass man and the only one around this bitch playing games is yo' ass," Mills fussed. "And if we're not together then why are you in your feelings about somebody who's claiming to be fucking me? I'm free to do whatever the fuck I want, right? You want to walk around this bitch like we ain't together and doing as you please, but then have a problem if I act accordingly. Shit don't work like that."

"You know what? Fuck you," she spat. "Don't be trying to flip it around because the fact still remains that you couldn't leave your females alone. You fine with having me in the shadows while you still messing with these duck ass hoes, so don't make it seem like you care. But I can't even blame you. This exactly what you wanted."

"Are you fucking serious right now?" His voice raised slightly. She had him seconds away from wanting to pull his dreads out. "How many times have I tried to tell your brothers about us, only for you to beg me not to? How many fucking times?"

"Preston, I really—" Trish moved around him in a hurry and rushed to the toilet just in time before the food she'd consumed earlier came hurling from her mouth.

"Yo, you good?" Mills asked with genuine concern as he held her hair out of the way.

When it seemed like she was finally finished, he moved to grab a washcloth from the shelf, so she could clean herself. She accepted it from him without meeting his gaze. He watched as she remained close to the toilet and pulled her knees to her chest.

"See, this what you get for stuffing your face with all that food earlier." Mills tried to lighten the mood.

"I know, right?" She avoided his gaze. "Can you get Taz for me?"

"Yeah. I'll be right back." He left her alone to go search for Taz.

Trish was glad to have him out of her presence and took that time to get her head together. This had been the norm for her for the last couple of weeks and it was driving her crazy. Almost every time she finished eating, she was heading to the bathroom soon after.

"What the hell you doing sitting next to the toilet looking all pitiful for?" Taz asked as she entered the bathroom with Kay and Mills right behind her.

"Baby, you're not looking too good. You might need to lie down for a minute," Kay suggested. Trish discreetly cut her eyes in Mills' direction. "Hey, Mills could you give us a minute?"

"Yeah. I'll be back to check on you, T." He kissed her forehead before leaving to give them privacy.

Once they were sure that he was completely out of the room, they started in with their interrogation. Trish wasn't ready to face the questions that she knew were coming.

"Bitch, this is the like third time in the last few weeks that I've caught your ass puking your guts out." Taz eyed her suspiciously. "You got something you want to tell us?"

"She better not." Kay's head whipped around in her direction. "T?"

"What, Kay?" Trish huffed,

"Don't *what* me," Kay said. "Answer the question. Is there something you need to be telling us or not?"

"Ughhh!" Trish dropped her head on her arms.

"I guess that's our answer right there." Taz shook her head. "Damn, T. How the hell did this happen?"

"How else does one get in this situation, Taz?" Trish snapped smartly.

"Nuh uh, hoe. Don't be trying to get mad at me because you were busting it open and now yo' ass facing the consequences," Taz retorted.

"So, what's next?" Kay asked.

"Nothing's next." Trish stood from the floor and smoothed her clothes out. "Nothing at all."

Trish tried to exit but was stopped by Taz's hand on her arm. "T, I already know what you're thinking. Don't go doing anything irrational," Taz pleaded.

"Taz, ain't nothing irrational about it. This is not what either of us need right now. We don't even know where we stand. Hell, I haven't even told my brothers about us. This would only make thing worse," Trish said sadly.

"T, right now is not the time to be worried about how Trae and Ty are going to feel. They'll get over it and you know they'll be there for you regardless." Taz wrapped her arm around Trish's shoulders. "Even though they may kill Mills."

"Ain't no doubt about that." Kay laughed. "At least you'll have all of us to help, because it'll be lights out for that nigga once this gets out."

"Well, thank you so much for that, Kay," Trish said sarcastically. "I feel so much better."

"But all jokes aside. Are you one-hundred percent sure?" Kay asked.

"Well, the five tests I took seemed to be pretty sure," Trish answered. "I planned on going to the doctor once we got back home."

"I can't wait that long," Taz said. "You know Sky has a doctor on call that comes here. You should see if you could get her to set something up."

"Hell no! Y'all see how they're all over her? She wouldn't even be able to get her doctor here without them being down her throat. I'll just wait," Trish objected. "And I don't want y'all to say a word to anybody. Not even Sky and Lay."

"We won't," they both vowed.

****

"Where did everybody disappear to?" Sky asked Trae as she approached him.

She was feeling a little dizzy earlier and decided to take a quick nap once lunch was over. Stacey and the triplets were still the only ones who knew of the pregnancy, so she fed Trae some story about her just being overwhelmed with everything. That wasn't completely false, but she knew that the baby played a big role. When she awakened, it seemed as though just about everyone had vanished.

"T's not feeling well, so she's upstairs sleep with Kay, while Bo's ass is somewhere eating again. Ty and Lay's nasty asses been locked away in their rooms, and Noc and Mills left a little while ago to run Taz to see the twins," Trae informed her.

"Okay." She kicked her shoes off beside the lounge chair he was occupying and climbed onto his lap, snuggling close to his body. "Any idea where my brother might be?"

"Ace and your crazy ass cousins are out back at the range," Trae answered. "They have a whole fucking gun range and training course out back."

Sky laughed at him. "Don't be acting like y'all don't have a gun range back home, too," Sky said.

"Yeah, at one of the warehouses. Not in the damn backyard." Trae laughed. "Taz was right. Y'all on some mafia shit for real around here."

"I wish you all would quit saying that mess," she said, hitting him in the chest.

"You gon' stop abusing me, girl." Trae pretended to be hurt, but she knew that was far from the truth. He probably barely felt those little licks. "I'm gon' start fighting your lil' ass back."

"Try me punk," Sky taunted.

"Oh, you think you bad now, huh?" Trae asked. "You must need a reminder of who's running shit."

"Nah, maybe you do though," Sky challenged.

Without warning, he stood and tossed her over his shoulder. A yelp escaped from Sky, causing her to quickly cover her mouth to suppress it. She was all laughs and giggles until she noticed that he was headed straight for the pool.

"Trae, you better not," she warned.

"Or what?" he asked, right before tossing her in. He jumped in right behind her, clothes and all.

"Ugh, I can't stand you," she fussed, wiping the water from her eyes.

"Shut up. You love me." He pulled her into his arms and began nibbling on her neck, moving his hands to remove the shirt that was now clinging to her body.

"What do you think you're doing?" she asked, stopping him.

"Helping you out of these wet clothes," he answered innocently.

"I don't think so," Sky said trying to back away from him. "You must want somebody to catch us?"

"No, but I've been sitting out here thinking about making love to you in this pool," Trae answered honestly while closing the space between them.

"No, Trae." Sky tried to stop him. "Not happening, so you might as well throw that little fantasy away. What's up with you and this lil' public sex obsession you got going on?"

"Sorry, but baby I can barely make out a thing you're saying with all this water in my ears," Trae said.

Trae picked her up and she instinctively wrapped her legs around his waist. He led them both over to the grotto at the opposite end of the huge pool. Once he had them comfortable, he grabbed her face in his hands and began to nibble on her lips, teasing her. Sky was growing impatient and began to whimper and wiggle in his lap.

"You want me, baby?" She nodded her head, but that wasn't good enough for him. "No, I need to hear you say it. You know better than that, mama."

"Yes, Trae. I want you," she answered breathlessly.

"You sure?" he checked.

"Trae," she whined.

He chuckled and began to remove their clothing. He was moving teasingly slow and it was driving Sky insane, but she knew that what was to come would be well worth it. It seemed to take him forever to undress them both and Sky was starting to lose her patience. Once the last article of clothing was removed, Sky hungrily attacked his mouth.

"Damn, baby." Trae chuckled. "I'm not going anywhere."

"Trae, I need you. Like right now," Sky told him.

She didn't wait for his reply. Instead, she took him into one of her small, delicate hands and guided him inside of her. They both let out appreciative moans. Sky had to take a moment to adjust to his size again. Trae was grateful for that because he too needed a moment to get himself together. She'd always felt amazing to him, but he didn't remember her feeling that damn good.

"Fuck," Trae groaned, dropping his head back as she slowly began to ride him. "This pussy keeps getting better and better."

It didn't take long before her body was shaking and convulsing around him. He lifted them both from the water and moved to a seated bench that had been tastefully, and conveniently, placed in the grotto.

"Damn, I've missed you," Trae admitted as he slid back into her from behind.

"Then show me." Sky moaned looking back at him. "Show me how much you missed me, baby."

Chapter 6

Stacey was sitting behind the desk in the office when there was a knock at the door. He paused what he was doing and called for whoever it was to enter.

"I'm not interrupting anything, am I?" Sky asked as she eased into the room and closed the door behind her.

"I've always dropped whatever I was doing for you. Nothing's changed, Sky Baby," he told her.

Sky nodded her head and took a seat in one of the armchairs in front of the desk. She was silent as she sat staring at him. Even though it had been a few days, she still hadn't gotten over the shock of her brother actually being alive and well.

"What's up, baby girl? Why you looking at me like that?" Stacey asked.

"Still can't believe you're here, Stace. It's just a lot to take in." Sky could feel herself getting choked up. "I really missed my big brother."

Stacey got up and rounded the desk, coming to stand in front of her. Taking both of her hands in his, he pulled her from the chair and into his arms. He knew the pain that she had to have felt, because he too experienced it when he'd first awakened from his coma and learned of her supposed death. That was the past now and he had no desire to continue thinking or talking about it, but he knew that Sky needed this moment. She needed time to adjust.

Sky had just gotten to the point where she wasn't having constant nightmares about Stacey. She even found herself being able to talk with Trae about him and share stories. Initially, it was hard for Sky to even speak his name without bursting into tears.

"I've missed you, too, Skylar." Stacey placed a kiss to her forehead.

They held their embrace for a few minutes more before Sky finally pulled away. Not that she really wanted to because she could spend the rest of her life in her brother's arms and be okay, but that wasn't why she came in there. They had business to discuss that couldn't wait.

"So Stace," she started. "You know we really need to talk, right?"

"What's up?" he asked going back to sit back behind the desk. He already knew what it was she wanted to discuss.

"Were you seriously going to bring me in?" she asked.

"Yeah, I was. Is that so hard to believe?" he asked.

"Hell yeah it is," she answered. "Come on, Stacey. You and Poppa treated me like some fragile ass little girl. Do you really expect me to believe that you wanted me beside you running an entire damn empire?"

"You know that's nowhere near the truth," Stacey disagreed. "Pops, may have tried to shield you from a lot, but I taught you every damn thing. He knew exactly what I was doing which was why he was so overprotective. Old man saw the same thing I saw, but he was in denial. I don't know how many times I have to say it, but this shit is in your blood. Always has been and you've proven that more than enough. You're built for this, Skylar."

"No, I'm not, Stacey. I'm not built for any of this. Yeah, I've learned a lot from you, but that's nothing. I can't do the shit that you and the rest of these ruthless ass people do," she told him.

"Who is this person right here? Because this damn sure isn't my Skylar sitting in front of me telling me what she can't do," Stacey said. "And what does being ruthless have to do with anything? That's my job. You have the brains and heart for this shit, baby girl."

Hesitation was written all over Sky's face. Not even a week ago she was just being held captive and talking about how she wanted nothing more than to be able to live a nice, normal life. Now, here she was contemplating taking her brother up on his offer to help run a drug empire. There wasn't anything nice and normal about that.

"Look, Skylar," Stacey said, grabbing her attention. "I know this is a lot and honestly I'm not even too sure about it anymore my damn self. I mean, you do have a little situation now and that's something to really consider. Along with Trae, being in Miami would be something to discuss."

"Neither of those reasons are why I'm hesitant about this, Stace," Sky told him. "There's just a lot of risks that I'm all too familiar with and can honestly live without."

"Those risks are there regardless." Stacey chuckled. "However you want to look at it, whenever you're directly involved or not, this shit is just as much yours as it is mines. That's automatic risk right there. Not to mention you're now with someone who's deep in the game. Trae and his people might not be on the same scale as our family, but that doesn't mean his name don't hold weight."

"I know all of that." She sighed.

"Baby girl, don't think I'm trying to pressure you into anything, because that's not the case. At the time, that decision felt right and I still stand by it," he told her. "But this is your life to live, Skylar. The decision isn't mines. I'll respect whatever you choose, because at the end of the day my only goal is for you to be straight."

"The fact still remains that I know nothing about running a drug business," Sky said.

"Really Skylar?" Stacey laughed. "Baby, the Santiago Empire is far from just drugs, and you know that. I have that covered. Stop being difficult, woman."

"Well, it ain't me if it's not difficult," she said, joining him in laughter. "Seriously, though. If I were to be on board with this, what exactly would I be doing?"

"I want you front and center with pretty much everything else. Pops had his hands in too many things to count, including a whole lot of international shit," Stacey revealed shaking his head.

STILL THUGGIN'

Sky sat and pondered on the opportunity that was presented to her. The only reason that she could come up with not to do was that it would be putting her at too much risk and make her a target. That wasn't much of a valid reason, because just like Stacey said, she was already one.

Hell, if she was going to be a target anyway, why not make it worth it. This was her family's legacy and it had almost been destroyed. It was time for them to make their presence known and show the world that the Santiago family was still standing and still a force to be reckoned with.

"I'm in," Sky said as she stood from her seat.

"Wait, what?" Stacey was shocked that she was actually on board. "I thought it would have taken a little more to convince you. Have you spoke with Trae about any of this?"

"No, but this is my decision to make. Either he's with it or he's not." Sky shrugged. "Family first."

"I understand that, but I also want you to take a moment to realize that *that* is your family now, too," he started. "Not only are y'all in a relationship, you're carrying that man's seed, Skylar. Don't take this the wrong way when I say this. I'm your brother, but I'm also a man and as a man I would be pissed if the soon-to-be mother of my child made a decision like this without even talking to me. That's not right and selfish on your part. You can't have that mentality, baby girl. Even if he's against it, you still have to do your part and at least communicate with the man."

"I planned on talking to him about it eventually, Stace. I still needed to come to you and see what was going on before I went to him anyways," she said. "I'm going to talk to him."

"Well, what you waiting on?" he questioned. "Get your butt out my office and go talk to him."

"Don't be trying to put me out. With yo' ugly self." Sky balled up a piece of paper and threw it at him.

"I'm just playing, baby. Your spoiled ass is welcome wherever I am," Stacey told her. "And you tried it lil' nigga. Ugly? Nah, you know your brother sexy as fuck."

"Boy, bye." Sky laughed. "You a'ight."

"Yeah whatever," he said getting up and meeting her at the door. "Go talk to him."

****

Sky and the rest of the ladies had decided to walk the grounds and ended up at one of the pavilions out back that faced the property's private beach. It had already begun to get late and there was a bit of a breeze because of their proximity to the water. They decided to like the fire pit that was position under the pavilion and all settled around it.

"It's so beautiful out here." Laiah admired the calming waters. "Makes me not even want to go back home."

"I swear," Taz agreed. "This is one thing I miss the most about living here. Y'all already know how much I love the water."

While they were all engaged in conversation, Trish noticed that Sky kept zoning out and not really there with them. She could tell by the stressed look on her face that Sky must have had a lot on her mind.

"Sky," Trish called, grabbing her attention. "What's wrong? You've been out of it over there."

"Oh, my bad. Nothing's wrong," Sky lied.

"Don't even think to sit over there lying to me, Sky. What's going on?" Trish pushed.

Sky released a heavy breath and sighed. "So much man. Just too much," Sky said shaking her head.

"Talk to me, baby." Trish moved to sit next to Sky.

"I don't even know where to start." Sky dropped her head on Trish's shoulder. "Y'all already know a little about everything that went on with me and my family. Well, of course Stacey is taking everything back over and he wants me beside him."

"Yeah, we found that bit of information out from Draya," Taz told her. "I'm still a lil' salty that you ain't been tell us about all of this though."

"I know, and I really am sorry about keeping y'all in the dark. To be honest, it's a lot that even I didn't know," Sky said.

"Have you thought about your brother's offer?" Trish questioned curiously.

"I told him yes," she answered.

"So, wait," Kay cut in. "Does that mean you're going to stay here in Miami?" Sky nodded her head.

"Of course I'm staying. I can't just walk away from my brother when he needs me. Yeah, Atlanta was nice and all, but this is where I belong."

"Whoa, Skylar," Trish said nudging her to sit up. "What did Trae have to say about all of this?"

"We haven't discussed any of this yet. It's not like he can make me go back. I care about your brother and wish things could be different, but my family comes first. I was—" She tried to explain before Trish cut her off.

"You kidding me, right?" Trish asked incredulously. "Because there's no way you're serious right now. That's selfish as hell of you. Now that you have your blood back, it's just fuck us? You wrong and you know it. Exactly when do you plan on saying something to Trae, Sky?"

"That's the same thing I want to know," Trae spoke from behind them.

All talking ceased. Sky really didn't want to turn around and face him. From the tone of his voice she could already tell that he had heard their conversation and wasn't happy. Sky looked on as Trish nervously looked between Sky and Trae. Sky couldn't really be upset with them because it's not like they knew that he would walk up on them in the middle of their conversation.

"Umm, we're going to head back up to the house and give you two some privacy," Trish hurriedly said and they all stood to walk away.

Sky still refused to look in Trae's direction and pleaded with her eyes for the women to stay. Trish mouthed an apology before rushing away. She knew her brother and she knew things were about to get ugly. That wasn't something she wanted to stick around for.

"Skylar," Trae called out to her.

She forced herself to look at him and immediately dropped her gaze after seeing the stern look that he had plastered on his face. This wasn't about to be an easy conversation and she honestly wasn't looking forward to it.

"When did you plan on telling me any of this?" he asked.

"I don't know, Trae," she answered with her voice barely above a whisper. "But I was going to tell you."

"Speak up and look at me when we're talking, ma," Trae ordered. "What type of shit you on, man?"

"I'm not on anything. I really was going to tell you. Whether you choose to believe that or not is on you," Sky told him.

Trae chuckled as he ran his hand over his head. This wasn't a humorous chuckle, though. This one was filled with malice. Sky had been around him enough to know that he did that when he was close to spazzing out.

"So, you planned on *telling* me, huh. Not sit down and discuss it with me or even ask how I felt about the shit? Just tell me?" he asked rhetorically. "Since when is it okay to do that shit?"

"Trae, I understand that you're upset but please realize that I'm grown and the decision was mines to make. I didn't need to seek your permission," she said, feeling herself becoming upset.

"Wow," Trae just stared at her. "Yeah, I realize something, alright. I realize that you're selfish and inconsiderate as fuck. It ain't about you seeking damn permission. It's about you at least acting like you give a damn about how the shit you do affects the people around you. But you're only worrying about yourself, Skylar. Just fuck the fact that you're in a whole damn relationship and your significant other might want to know that you're trying to move to a completely different state, right?"

"You're making things seem way worse than what they really are, Trae." Sky sighed.

"Man, forget it." Trae threw his hands up. "If you still don't get where I'm coming from then just fuck it. Do you, man. I'm glad that you're safe and reunited with your family and all that good shit, but it's time for me to take my ass back to the A."

"Trae," Sky called after him as he walked away. "Trae!"

He continued to ignore her and headed towards the main house so that he could notify everyone to get prepared for their departure. There was really no point in him sticking around. He was genuinely happy that Sky was safe, and he felt confident knowing that she was in good hands with her folks. It was just time for him to leave before he ended up doing or saying something that he might regret later.

Never would he have figured that Sky could be so selfish. He didn't know if she was just feeling herself now or not, but he hoped that she wouldn't just disregard everything that he and his family had been doing for her since she'd entered their lives. Trae loved her.

Hell, they all did. Her way of thinking was really messing with him right now, so his best option right now was to leave or else someone's feelings were bound to get hurt.

Chapter 7

"That's just it? You're really going to go like this, Trae?" Trish asked as she watched her brother prepare to leave. "I know that shit was kind of messed up, but don't just walk away like this. At least talk to her and hear the girl out. She didn't—"

"What the fuck I need to hear her out for?" Trae barked. "T, she made her decision. Instead of being a woman about it, she couldn't even come to me. It ain't like I could've forced her ass to come back to Atlanta if she didn't want to. All I'm saying is that her inconsiderate ass could have at least pretended to give a damn about me and this relationship. But I ain't even trippin'. I'm good on her."

Noc shook his head as he leaned against the passenger side of one of their awaiting trucks. He could tell just by the way Trae was acting that Sky's actions had really hurt him.

"Trae, you don't—" Trish tried to reason, but Trae cut her off before she could finish.

"T, I love you, but you need to drop that shit," Trae told her as he checked a notification that came through his phone. "And quit trying to stall and finish getting your stuff."

"I really don't understand why we can't just stay here. I'm not trying to leave her right now," Trish told him.

"T-Baby, I've already compromised enough as it is and I'm not moving on this. Either y'all go with the twins or you leave with me. Either way, you're not fucking staying *here* without us," Trae told her sternly. "Now hurry up."

Trish turned in a huff and headed back inside to finish getting her things. Everyone else had already gotten their belongings and had them ready to load into the cars. Trish was still dragging the process on because she hoped that her brother would change his mind. She knew that was wishful thinking, though. Trae was as stubborn as they came. When his mind was made up, there was no changing it.

She couldn't really blame him in this situation, because she felt that Sky could have handled everything a lot better than what she did. There was no point in dwelling on that now because what was done was done. Trish just wished that Trae would have at least taken a second to calm down and get his thoughts together instead of reacting off emotions. Now, they had an even bigger mess on their hands.

The love that Trae had for Sky was very obvious and anyone with eyes could see it. It was a shame that things between them had taken such a drastic turn for the worse. Even Stacey had tried to intervene and talk to Trae, but he wasn't trying to hear any of it.

Trae's only focus right now was getting away from Sky and back to his money.

"This shit crazy," Bo said to Mills as they approached the truck to place the women's bags in the trunk. "We went through all of that shit just for these two stubborn motherfuckers to break up. Hell nall. They better take a few days, sleep this shit off, and make up."

"Bruh, shut the fuck up," Mills said as he pushed past him.

"Bitch, don't be pushing me. I'm just saying though," Bo told him. "All of this just to break up over some bullshit? That nigga better hop out his feelings."

"Nigga, didn't he just tell yo' ass to be quiet?" Ty questioned. "He got every right to be in his feelings."

"I'm not saying he don't, because I know I would have put my foot in Kay's ass if she tried to pull some shit like that." Bo laughed. "But look at the bigger picture. We're talking about a fucking empire here, man. Not just drugs or none of that petty shit, my nigga. Fucking weaponry, international shit, businesses all across the fucking globe, and who knows what else! And his lady's running shit? Man, fuck where she wants to stay. If she wanted to move to fucking Japan that nigga should have been with it."

"Shut your simple ass up and don't worry about what the fuck I do, nigga," Trae spat as he approached them.

Noc approached him and dapped hands with him. "You good?" he asked Trae.

"Yeah, man. Y'all acting like the world ending or something. It is what it is," Trae said and looked back towards the door to find

Trish still taking her precious time. "T, stop dragging your damn feet and bring your ass!"

"Nigga, don't rush me," she yelled back. She turned back and pulled Sky into her arms. "Me and Taz are staying down here a few more days with the twins, so we'll definitely be back. I don't understand why his stubborn ass making us leave anyway."

"It's okay, T. You know how your brother is," Sky said sadly. "I just hope we can remain close after all of this."

"Nuh uh, heifer. You acting like this gon' change anything between us. I had you first anyway," Trish said as she pulled away from her. "I'll try to talk to my big-headed brother. But regardless of if y'all difficult asses work it out or not, you're still my damn sister. Play with it if you want to, Skylar."

Sky laughed. "No need to threaten me, baby."

"Better not be," Trish said. "I'll call you once we get settled."

****

"Stop with all that damn sulking," Stacey told Sky. "I told yo' ass that you were wrong for how you handled the shit."

"Okay, Stace. I know that, so I don't need you to keep saying it," she snapped at him.

"Don't get your lil ass beat in here, Skylar," Stacey warned. "I don't know what you mad at me for. You were talking big shit earlier. It's time to suck it up, put on your big girl panties, and fix it."

"Fuck him," Julio chimed in. "If he's so quick to leave her over something like this, then she's better off without him anyways."

"O, shut the hell up," Josiah told him. "Whether they like it or not, they both need to figure something out because they have a kid to consider."

"Right," Jonas cosigned.

Julio waved them both off. "I'm not trying to hear it. That should have been all the more reason for him to stay. That might be the real reason why he tucked his tail and ran."

"Yeah, if he even knew about a damn baby," Stacey grilled Sky. "Did he, Skylar?"

He got his answer when she avoided his gaze and dropped her head. She knew that Stacey was about to rip her a new one. He had been constantly pushing her to tell Trae about the baby every chance he got, but Sky was too afraid.

"Why the hell didn't you tell him, Skylar?" Stacey raised his voice. "And don't try to give me some lame excuse either."

"Because I wasn't ready to tell him," she yelled at him. She got up from her seat and left them all sitting there.

"I sure hope you plan on keeping her behind the scenes until this whole pregnancy thing is over," Jonas said. "She's been very temperamental and all over the place. We don't need her erratic in meetings, blowing people's shit off just because she's feeling hormonal."

"Fuck you, Jo!" Sky yelled from what they assumed was the kitchen.

"She must not be too upset. Sounds like she's in there about to tear the kitchen up." Josiah laughed as they listened to Sky loudly rummaging through the cabinets.

"I'm not about to deal with her shit today." Stacey sighed as he ran his hand down his face. "Skylar, bring your spoiled behind back in here! We're not finished!"

"Yes, the hell we are if y'all are just going to continue to sit here and talk about how much I messed things up," Sky fussed as she entered back into the sitting room with them.

"We have bigger issues to deal with right now that are far more important than that petty shit you have going on," Stacey told her. "You get a pass this once, but this is the only time I'm going to say anything to you about keeping your damn emotions in check! You know better than that!"

Skylar rolled her eyes and mumbled something under her breath, causing Julio to snicker to himself. "Speak up! I can't hear you," Stacey barked.

"Nothing, Stacey! Damn," Sky said irritably.

"This shit right here is exactly what had me second-guessing my decision. Ain't no room for all this emotional ass shit in this business. That's a sign of weakness and the moment you show that to these big boys out here, they're going to use it to their advantage," Stacey lectured. "There's a time and a place for all of that and right now ain't the time. So, put that mess to the side, because we have a lot that needs to be handled."

"Gotcha," Sky replied with a blank expression.

"Good," Stacey nodded. "Now first order of business, I think it's about time that we make our presence known and let the world know that we're back."

****

Trae and the crew, minus Trish and Taz, had been back in Atlanta for less than five full hours and were already regretting returning. As a result of everything that went on because of the beef with Slim and Jayceon, any and everything else had pretty much been put on the backburner.

"Aye, man. We 'bout to head out and run through the spots to see how shit's been holding up," Mills informed Trae. "You know these niggas think it's a party when the boss ain't around."

"Oh yeah," Trae agreed. "And tell them niggas it's double time. But let me dip up out of here. I got some shit I need to see about, but I'll get up with y'all boys later tonight to run them numbers."

"We got you, man," Bo said as he headed to his car.

Trae and Ty both headed in the direction of Trae's car and got in. There had been so much stuff demanding their attention that it hardly left room to think about anything else. Trae didn't too much mind the distraction, though. Anything to take his mind away from Sky was welcomed.

Trish swore up and down that he was completely overreacting and wrong for just walking away from Sky. That's not how Trae saw things. It was much bigger to him. The entire ordeal made Trae realize a lot of things, including the fact that Sky wasn't ready to accept the type of love that Trae was trying to give. He wasn't about to drag around sulking about it, though. Hell, no. It was just time to say "fuck it" and bring the old Trae back.

"Nigga, what you over there in deep thought about?" Ty asked, interrupting his thoughts.

"Just how shook the city about to be now that the old Trae is back," Trae answered.

"The old Trae?" Ty questioned with a raised brow. "The fuck does that mean, bruh?"

"Exactly what I said." Trae shrugged. "I tried to cool it and chill since I was trying to do that relationship shit but fuck it. It's back to 'Money over bitches and family over everything' for me. Fuck everything else."

"If you don't shut that dumb shit you talking up. You ain't never been on no dumb reckless shit before and you ain't about to start now. Don't even play. You already know that you and sis going to work this shit out. Y'all stubborn asses get on my fucking nerves, man," Ty fussed as they pulled up to his home.

"I'm good," Trae simply said. "Get yo' ugly ass out my whip, nigga."

"Fuck you, crybaby." Ty laughed as he got out and went to check his mailbox.

Trae had already exited the car and was waiting by the door waiting for Ty to unlock it. Trae had his own key to Ty's house, but he never used it unless there was a need to. Ty was sifting through the various pieces of mail until he came across an envelope that made his movements still instantly.

"Come on, man. It's cold as shit out here," Trae complained. "What you standing there looking crazy for?"

Trae watched as Ty's nostrils began to flare as he read over the paper in his hands. He ignored Trae's confused stare and walked past him and unlocked the door, before entering and heading straight to his den and to the bar.

"What the hell's up with you?" Trae asked concerned.

Ty remained quiet as he downed a shot on Jack Daniels and slid the papers he had been reading over to Trae. Trae's eyes scanned over the paper in his hands and tried to keep his cool. That was a hard task to do, considering what he had just read.

"What is this shit, Tyree?" Trae barked.

"What the fuck does it look like?" Ty barked back. "You just read the exact same thing I did."

Trae began to pace in front of the bar in deep thought. He definitely wasn't prepared to return home to this type of news. This was the last thing he would have expected, and it couldn't have come at an even more fucked up time.

"I'm telling you right now when I cross paths with that bitch, she's dead," Trae declared.

Ty dragged both hands down his face. Trae's response was no surprise to him. This had been his stance from the beginning. If Trae had it his way, she would have never even seen this inside of the jail and instead, would be at the bottom of somebody's river in a body bag. Their "mother" got a pass because he was young at the time and there wasn't much he could have done.

"We can't go flying off the handle with this. You know how your mother is and the bitch is slick," Ty tried to reason.

Trae swiftly moved the stand directly in Ty's face. "Don't ever refer to that bitch as my mother again. That bitch ain't shit to me! She ain't give a damn about being our mother when she tried to kill our asses, so that don't mean shit to me, now."

"You know I don't give a damn about her, but all I'm saying is we have to be smart with whatever we do," Ty offered. "Don't go reacting off emotion. Think man."

"I have thought about it." Trae grabbed his keys from the bar. "For the last fifteen years, if we're being technical, and the bitch is dead."

Chapter 8

"Hey, man. I've been calling you all day trying to check on you and your ass ain't answered or tried to call me back not once," Mills spoke to Trish's voicemail. "Don't play with me, T. I'm really trying to be patient with you right now. Call me the fuck back."

Frustrated, he ended the call and tossed his phone on the bar. Mills had been trying to reach Trish since they made it back to Atlanta, but she still wasn't taking his calls or replying to any of his messages. He knew that she saw him calling because she answered the phone for Trae with no problem. This right here was the type of stuff that pissed him off. She was quick to try to point the finger at him and say that he was the one playing games, but she was the queen of games.

"Fam, who got you over here mad at the world?" Bo laughed. "Throwing your phone and shit."

"I'm so damn tired of these females, bruh." Mills sighed.

"I hope like hell you ain't stressing about that trifling ass so-called baby mama of yours because I just saw that bitch over at the trap," Bo told him. "Smiling in that nigga Lil' Jon's face."

"I ain't worried about that hoe." Mills waved him off.

"Good, because it's gon' be like an episode of Maury 'round this bitch when she finally have that baby. Ain't no telling whose seed that is." Bo shook his head.

"I'm already hipped," Mills told him. "Her thot ass needs to stop going around telling people it's mine. Knowing damn well that's a lie."

"Shid, you fucked her, so it might be." Bo laughed.

"Nigga, don't be trying to act like you weren't bussing that down, too," Mills challenged. "The only reason she ain't out screaming your name is because she ain't trying to get that ass tagged by Kay."

"Oh yeah?" Bo smirked. "I don't think that's it, because T's just as lethal with it."

Mills stopped what he was doing and looked at Bo. "Nigga, what does T have to do with anything?"

"Don't even try to play me," Bo said. "So, you and T ain't been fucking around?"

"Man, what you talking about?" Mills asked with a straight face.

"Bruh, you might as well cut all that shit out because I know. My question is, when the hell did this shit start? Hell, how did it start?" Bo asked.

"Kay ass can't hold water." Mills shook his head.

"Nah, nigga. Don't be trying to blame her. You gave yourself away, she just confirmed it," Bo told him.

"How exactly did I do that?" Mills wanted to know.

"A lot just makes sense now. Plus, it was obvious by the way you were cutting up at that table when we were in Miami. I know you, nigga," Bo said. "And so do them niggas, so I really wouldn't be surprised if they picked up on that shit, too. But then again, I doubt it because they would have already tried to kill your ass. Now, answer my question."

"Almost a year and I don't know how this shit happened," Mills told him. "It just did and now her ass got me all fucked up in the head."

"Well you need to be figuring something out because it's gon' be hell once they find out," Bo told him right before Trae and Ty walked into the club.

Trae had decided for all of them to meet there since he already had to meet with his contractors. He wasn't wasting any time with remodeling the club and getting it back up and running. The fire had been started on the left side of the building and luckily for him the firemen were able to get a handle on it before it spread throughout the rest of the structure.

"What's up, boss man?" Bo greeted Trae as he gave both he and Ty dap.

"Let's go to the back," Trae told them.

Once they were all situated in Trae's office, he began to update them on everything. Now with Santana out of the picture, he needed a new connect. With the way his men moved work, his stash wouldn't last him more than a few months.

"So are you pulling out of Miami?" Ty questioned. "We have a good lil' bit of money tied up down there."

"For right now, I'm not trying to fuck with Miami until I figure out what I'm about to do about this connect," Trae told them. "I can't even fuck with Elias. His ass already knew what was about to go down and with Ace being back, Hern ain't about to let Elias do shit in Miami. He's not trying to have those problems."

"I know you don't want to, but you need to get at that nigga Ace," Ty told him. "Fuck all that personal shit. It's about to be damn near impossible to get anything without eventually going through them or their people anyways. Especially if we trying to get that type of quality."

"Let me worry about that," Trae said. "We're good right now. I'll deal with that when we get there."

The ringing of Trae's office phone brought their conversation to a halt. He picked up and listened to what the caller was saying. When he was done, he turned to Mills and shook his head while laughing.

"Man, if you don't go and get that crazy ass girl from in front of my club, I'm gon' put a bullet in her ass," Trae told him.

"What? Who?" Mills asked, confused.

Trae turned on his camera monitors and pointed to where Porsha was standing out front giving his staff a hard time. They watched as she threw her hands around, rolling her neck. There was no sound, but just from the look of things they could tell that she was yelling.

"I'm about to kill this bitch," Mills seethed as he got up from his seat and left the room.

"Just don't do that shit in front of my club," Trae called to his back while laughing. "How he even get caught up with that hoodrat?"

As soon as Mills made it outside, he snatched her up by her arm and moved her away from the front of the club.

"Get your damn hands off of me," Porsha yelled, trying to snatch her arm away from him.

"Yo, what the hell is your problem?" Mills yelled back. "And what you doing coming down here for in the first place?"

"Nigga, I'm not the one with the problem," she spat. "If you would be a man and handle your responsibilities, I wouldn't have a reason to show up down here. I've been trying to get in touch with you for the past month and you act like you can't answer! Anything could have been wrong with me and your child!"

"First of all, stop saying that that's my damn child," Mills barked. "And I already told your simple ass not to call me until the baby's born!"

"Really, Mills?" she asked like he had hurt her feelings or something. "I know who I slept with and I know who my child's father is! When it comes out that she's yours you're going to feel like a straight up fool for how you treated me and the fact that you're missing out on this entire pregnancy. The baby ain't even here and you're already a damn deadbeat!"

Mills moved swiftly to stand in her face. "Don't ever fix your mouth to call me a deadbeat," he spoke through gritted teeth. "*If* that is my child, I have no problem being there and taking care of it. If its mother wasn't such a hoe, I wouldn't have anything to question and we wouldn't be going through this shit!"

"I wasn't such a hoe when you were between my legs, now was I?" she asked with her arms folded across her chest.

Mills laughed in her face. "Actually, you were," he told her. "Look, I'm not about to continue going through this shit with you. You right. I laid down with your trifling ass so there is a possibility that it could be my seed."

"Ain't no could be, nigga," Porsha interrupted him.

"Shut the fuck up and let me talk," he scolded her. She rolled her eyes but didn't say anything else. "Like I was saying. There is a possibility that it's mine. A very small one, but still a possibility. I don't want you calling me or popping up unless it's an emergency that has something to do with this damn baby and its wellbeing. Other than that, stay yo' ass away from me."

"What about doctor's appointments?" she questioned. "So, you don't even want to know how the baby's doing or even see it for yourself? That falls under the category of wellbeing."

"What I need to go to appointments for? Just update me on how shit going," Mills told her.

"I bet if this was you and that bitch's Trish's baby that you would make sure to take your black ass to every appointment," she snapped nastily.

"But it ain't, now is it?" Mills asked her.

"I wonder what Trae would say if he knew his boy was smashing his little sister." Porsha smirked. "He's fucked plenty of niggas up for less. That's like the ultimate betrayal right there."

Before she could react, Mills' large hand had found its way around her neck and he had her pressed against the building. Her eyes widened in fear at the look in his eyes. She knew that she was teetering on a thin line with her taunting.

"Keep fucking playing with me, Porsha. I will body your lil' ass and you know that," he spoke close to her ear.

Mills felt a hand on his shoulder. "Bruh, let her go," Bo told him.

Mills continued to look at her for a few seconds longer before he finally released her. She dramatically grabbed at her sore throat gasping for air.

"Are you crazy?" She coughed, dramatically heaving for air. "I'm pregnant and you're just going to choke me like that? You could have fucking killed me!"

"If I wanted to kill you, you'd be dead," Mills said and turned to walk away. "Take your ass home and when I call you better answer the fucking phone."

"I didn't drive here. Mesha dropped me off," Porsha stuttered.

"You really trying me, man." Mills sighed.

"Yo, I can drop her ass off. We don't need you killing the bitch," Bo offered.

"Nah, I got it," Mills assured him. "Let them know I'm out. I'll get up with y'all later after I handle this shit."

"You sure?" Bo asked skeptically.

"Positive," Mills confirmed and then turned to Porsha. "Get your ass in the car!"

****

"Nay, she's gorgeous," Taz swooned as she held her niece in her arms. "You must have been arguing with Von this whole pregnancy because she looks just like his ugly ass."

"Girl, don't play yourself. You know a nigga nice," Tavon said as he reached to take his daughter from Taz's arms.

"Nooo, Von. I just got her," Taz whined as she turned away from him so he couldn't get her. "You can get her back when we leave."

"How you gon' come in here and try to hog my baby?" He laughed.

"So, what's her name?" Trish asked.

"Tavona Grace Martez," Nay answered proudly.

Taz and Tavon were still fighting over who would hold the baby when Tamar walked in the house. "Yo, where my niece at?" he asked as soon as he rounded the corner.

Nay laughed and shook her head as she watched the three siblings battling over her daughter. She could already see that this little girl was about to be beyond spoiled.

"I'm gon' pray for you, honey." Trish laughed. "They're about to have her spoiled rotten."

"Ugh, I already know it," Nay agreed. "Von's been all over her since we got home from the hospital. He's so obsessed with her little butt that his ass barely even lets me hold her. When he does, it's usually just to eat and he be right there in my face the entire time watching, with his annoying ass."

"You just gon' talk about me like I ain't standing right here? Remember that, Nay." Tavon laughed.

Trish sat and laughed at the two going back and forth. She admired the love that the two of them shared. Tavon was about the only one amongst her brothers and cousins who was never into running through females. He and Nay had been together since their junior year in high school and were still going strong. Yes, they had their problems, but they always came out on top and better than before.

That's the type of love that Trish wanted for herself. As much as she would like to have that with Mills, she was afraid to give herself to him completely. She had known him just about all her life and knew firsthand how he was with females.

Even that didn't stop her from wanting him. She constantly fought with herself on whether she should put him out of her misery and call him back. Maybe it was just this baby that had her all in her feelings, but one minute she wanted to put a bullet in his ass and the next she wanted nothing more than to be wrapped in his arms.

Trish got up from the couch and walked to the kitchen so that she could have some privacy. She stood staring at her phone in her hand trying to decide whether she wanted to make the call. After a few minutes of debating, she finally worked up enough courage to dial his number. Her nerves were all over the place as she waited for him to answer. Just as she was about to hang up, the phone was answered.

"Hello," Trish spoke after a few seconds of silence. "Preston?"

"Who's this?" Porsha questioned with an attitude.

"Nah, the question is who the hell this is?" Trish snapped. "Where's Mills?"

"Honey, you're the one that called my man's phone, so I don't really think you have the right to be asking questions," Porsha said smartly.

"I just know this ain't scary ass Porsha trying to talk big shit over the phone," Trish laughed. "Now like I said, where's Mills?"

"Nall, like I said, you don't have the right to be questioning my man's whereabouts," Porsha said and hurriedly disconnected the phone.

Trish sat her phone on the counter and tried her best to calm herself down. Mills must have really lost his damn mind. He had been constantly blowing her phone up, but the moment he made it back to Atlanta he was back in his baby mother's face. This was making her decision about what she was going to do about the baby a whole lot easier. If he wanted to play it like that then she would play right along with him.

Chapter 9

Sky stood at the front entrance as she waited for the car to make its way up the estate's long driveway. Trish and Taz were exiting the back of the car before it even came to a complete stop. Sky wished that Kay and Laiah could have stayed, but she understood that there was a lot that need to be done back in Atlanta. Besides, Bo and Ty weren't going for them staying down in Miami without them anyways. It was also obvious that Mills wasn't too fond on Trish's decision to stay behind but there wasn't much he could say about it.

"Hey, mama," Trish greeted as she hugged Sky.

Taz, along with the twins, were right behind her. After Taz finished with her hug, Trish turned to introduce Sky to the twins.

"Sky, this is Tamar and Tavon. Y'all, this is Trae's future wife Skylar," Trish introduced.

"Really, T?" Sky asked while shaking her head. She turned her attention back to the twins. "Nice to finally meet y'all."

"If it ain't the damn Terrible Two," Stacey joked from behind them. "How y'all boys been?"

"Damn, man," Tamar said as he and Stacey shared a brotherly hug. "This shit crazy, Ace. I know they said you were alive, but it's different seeing it for myself."

"Crazy ain't the word," Stacey said as he moved to greet Tavon in the same manner. "Heard you just had a lil' one. Congrats, bro."

"Thanks, fam," Tavon said with a proud smile on his face. "It's a small ass world. I still can't believe the same person Trae's ass been going crazy about is your damn sister."

"Yeah, well they both lucky that I actually like Trae's ass or else that would have been shut down the moment I touched down." Stacey laughed.

Sky rolled her eyes in Stacey's direction and shook her head. He swore up and down he was running something, but they both knew she had him wrapped around her finger. Always had and that wasn't about to change now.

"We need to holler at you about a few things, too," Tamar told him. "That's if you're not too busy."

"Nah, I got a little time," Stacey told him. "Come on."

She grabbed Trish and Taz's hands and led them inside so that the three of them could have their own time. She wasn't sure how long they would be staying. Knowing Trac, he probably gave them a time limit.

"Where are those fine ass cousins of yours?" Trish asked the moment she made herself comfortable in one of the loungers by the pool.

"Somewhere minding their business," Sky told her. "T, I'm not going to tell your fast ass again to leave my cousins alone."

"I can't stand a stingy hoe." Trish laughed. "I just wanted to say hey. Ain't no harm in that."

"Don't play. You be eye-fucking Ju every time his butt is anywhere near you, T," Sky said. "I don't have time for those problems that we both know will come from that."

"She thinks she's slick," Taz chimed in. "Only reason she be doing that mess is to make Mills jealous."

"Fuck, Preston," Trish snapped. "Ain't nobody thinking about his trifling behind. Me looking at Julio's fine ass ain't got a damn thing to do with that nigga."

"Whoa," Sky said, looking at Trish curiously. "Why all the animosity?"

"I know right," Taz said. "What's up with y'all confused butts now?"

"Nobody's confused. I'm just good on his ass," Trish told them, right before her phone began vibrating in her purse again. "And I bet money that's his ugly ass blowing me up for the millionth time."

"What happened?" Sky asked.

"He sits up here and does all this talking about how he wants to be with me and how he's tired of hiding this, but I damn sure can't tell. First, you get this raggedy heifer pregnant and swear up and down it ain't yours. Got this mop bucket head hoe approaching me like she's some damn body. If the bitch ain't nobody and they ain't got nothing going on, then why the hell is she answering his phone?

The minute I'm not around he runs right to the bitch. She gon' have the nerve to tell me that it ain't my place to be questioning *her* man's whereabouts," Trish ranted. "What type of shit is that? When I see them, I'm fucking both of 'em up on sight."

Sky and Taz both sat looking at her. Instead of sitting like she had been, she was now in front of them pacing. They knew she must have been pretty pissed off about the entire situation because she was still mumbling obscenities to herself.

"Have you talked to him?" Sky finally spoke, breaking her out of her trance.

"Hell no," Trish snapped. "What we need to talk about? She did enough talking for him."

Just like clockwork, her phone began vibrating again. Trish stopped pacing and glared at her purse. The way she was staring at it, Sky was surprised that the damn thing didn't catch fire.

"Just see who it is, T," Taz urged. "It could be one of your brothers. You know we were supposed to call them and Trae's probably acting a fool by now."

Trish reluctantly dug in her purse until she was able to locate her phone. Instead of Mills calling like she had assumed, Kay's name flashed across her screen.

"What you want, lady?" Trish answered.

"So, I got to do all this to get your ass on the damn phone?" Mills barked through the phone.

"Well maybe you should take the hint and stop calling," Trish sassed.

"You and that slick ass mouth of yours gon' make me fuck you up. What you doing all this childish shit for anyway? I'm sitting here busting my ass trying to make things right with us and you steady on bullshit," Mills fussed, but she had long tuned him out once she saw the triplets emerging on four-wheelers from the far end of the estate's massive yard.

Everything that Mills was saying was going in one ear and out the other. They had already dismounted their rides and were headed their way. The powerful strides of Julio's long legs had her in a trance. Granted, all three brothers were damn near identical, they all had their own uniqueness about them. Something about Julio's aura drew her more to him. It didn't take much for Trish to conclude that Julio was more of the trouble-making hothead out of the three. Whereas Josiah was more the calm and authoritative one, and Jonas just went with the flow.

"You don't hear me talking to you?" Mills yelled, catching her attention.

By now the triplets had made it over to them. Josiah and Jonas greeted the ladies before continuing into the house. Julio, on the other hand, decided to stick around. He swooped down to give Sky a hug and a kiss on her forehead, before moving to Taz to give her a hug as well.

"Yeah, I hear you," Trish spoke, while locking eyes with Julio. "I just ain't listening to a damn thing you're saying."

Julio was now approaching her and moved in to hug her. "How are you today, beautiful?" he spoke with a smirk plastered on his face.

Julio knew what he was doing. He was almost certain that the person on the phone was Mills. His tone was very low and intimate, but still loud enough so that the caller could hear him clearly. Sky just rolled her eyes and shook her head, because she, too, could see exactly what his slick ass was doing.

Mills menacing laugh came flowing through the line. Trish knew what that laugh meant, but she was too pissed off to even care. "So, you call yourself fucking with that motherfucker? That's what we do now?" he questioned in an even tone.

"If I am messing with him, that's of no concern to yo' ass. Worry about you and your bitch, because she made it perfectly clear to me that you're no longer a concern of mines," Trish said coolly. "You can get off my line now."

Trish disconnected their call and placed her phone back in her purse. Julio was standing in front of her flashing that million-dollar smile of his, while Sky was off to the side looking at them both.

"I'm telling you now, T," Sky started. "If some bullshit gets started because of you, I'm kicking yo' behind."

"I'm not worried about Preston's butt," Trish said, waving Sky off. She was still focused on Julio.

"And you shouldn't be, beautiful. Not as long as I'm around," Julio assured her, before winking at her and leaving to join his brothers inside.

STILL THUGGIN'

****

Things at the club were surprisingly progressing at a quick pace. Within the next three weeks or so, the club would be back up and running like nothing ever happened. Trae was thankful for that because the club had turned out to be a major money-maker for him. He hadn't really been expecting it to become so popular so fast.

"Hey Trae," Laiah greeted after he answered his office line. "You need to come do this interview."

"Interview? What I need to do an interview for? All that's on you," Trae told her.

"Which is exactly what I just tried to explain to her, but obviously she ain't really comprehending that," Laiah said with her voice filled with aggravation. "And this lil' attitude she got ain't really helping her case."

"Whoa, calm down," Trae instructed.

Trae ran a hand down his face. He did not feel like dealing with this right now, but he also knew that Laiah's patience was wearing thin. His best bet was to diffuse the situation before it had the chance to get out of hand.

"I'm about to head down there," Trae said before disconnecting the call.

Trae already knew where this was about to go. There should be no reason for this person to insist on him doing the interview instead of Laiah, when she was the damn manager. The last thing

Trae wanted to do was entertain a groupie who was only using the job as a way the get close to him.

Once he stepped off the private elevator, he noticed Laiah standing behind the bar with one of the bartenders, checking their inventory. She looked up when she heard the elevator and nodded in the direction that his guest was waiting.

The first thing Trae noticed was the woman's long shapely legs and round fat bottom that looked to be fighting to get out of the tight, short skirt she had squeezed in—definitely not attire for an interview. The constant shifting she was doing led Trae to believe that the six-inch pumps that she was wearing must not have been too comfortable. He shook his head and headed to approach her so that he could get this over with.

"You're here for the interview, correct?" Trae questioned from behind her, startling her.

"Oh, God. You scared me," she said grabbing her chest. "I didn't even hear you walk up. But yes, I'm here for the interview."

"You do understand that it's the manager's job to conduct all interviews right?" Trae questioned, pointing towards Laiah.

"Yes, I understand that, but I know for a fact she doesn't like me," she replied innocently. "So, I figured my best bet would be to interview with the boss man."

"See, that's something we don't need around here. You might want to go ahead and leave now if you're not able to leave personal issues at the door," Trae informed her. "Otherwise, let's get this interview started, please."

Trae motioned towards one of the booths for her to take a seat. Once they were both situated comfortably, Trae began the interview.

"And excuse my manners. I'm Trae Martez, the owner," Trae said. "I didn't get your name."

"Honey," she answered, extending her hand out across the table to him.

"Well, *Honey*," Trae said. "Is that your real name?"

"Um, no. It's Latissa," she told him.

"Then that's what I'll call you," Trae told her. "Listen, Latissa. I know this is a club and all, but you still need to treat this interview with the same professionalism that you would any other job. Understand?"

"Oh, I'm sorry Trae. I just—" His raised hand cut her off.

"Mr. Martez," Trae corrected her.

Latissa's cheeks flushed red with embarrassment. She hadn't thought that he would be this hard. One of her friends who already worked at the club painted a completely different picture of Trae. She kept going on and on to Latissa about how fine her boss was and how much of a ladies' man he was. That alone had Latissa curious and confident that she could handle her task. Men loved her, and she hadn't come across one yet who was able to resist her. But Trae Martez had definitely shook the game up.

Latissa hadn't really expected their first meeting to go down like this. He wasn't being rude or anything, but his demeanor was not one that was friendly. Straight business. He hadn't broken eye contact not once and that surprised Latissa even more. Her huge double-d cup breasts were practically spilling from the tight blouse she wore, but there hadn't been one glance from him.

Hell, if she would have known getting his attention was going to be this hard, she would have gone ahead and let Laiah interview her and just worked her way to Trae once she got the job. The way things were going already had her feeling like she might not even get the job.

After a few more questions from Trae, they were finally concluding the interview. Latissa couldn't really tell what Trae was thinking because his expression had been neutral the entire time. She held her breath as she waited for what he would say next.

"Okay, Latissa," Trae said, bringing her attention back to their conversation. "We have a pretty solid staff here already, but it shouldn't be a problem fitting you in. There's always a need for girls working the floor. Once your probationary period is over, you'll be able to be put in the rotation for servicing our VIP area. Is that okay with you?"

"That's fine with me. I'm just thankful for this opportunity and ready to work," she answered excitedly. "When's the reopening?"

"We'll be sending a memo out to staff once everything is finalized and there's a definite date," Trae informed her. "But before you do anything, you need to get with Laiah so that you can handle whatever paperwork she has and get your sizes to her for uniforms. Trish, the other manager, is away on business at the moment, but both she and Laiah are the club's managers and should be who you report to for anything."

Trae didn't miss the look that flashed across her face at the mention of Trish's name. She had already crossed paths with Laiah, Trish, and Kay a few times in the past and they weren't her biggest fans. Knowing that she would now have to answer to Trish and Laiah didn't sit well with her, but she wasn't about to let that show. She quickly tried to fix herself once she noticed that Trae had more than likely caught on to her facial expression.

"Will that be a problem?" he asked.

"No, not at all," she quickly assured him.

"Well if that's all, we can wrap things up here," Trae said standing from the booth and extending his hand to her. "Remember to see Laiah before you leave."

With that, he walked away and stopped to say a few words to Laiah before heading back in the direction of the elevator. Latissa kept her eyes on him the entire time until he was out of her sight.

"Good lawd! That man knows he fine," Latissa spoke to herself. "I'm gon' make sure that I make his sexy ass mines. Just watch."

She was so caught up in her thoughts of Trae that she hadn't even realized that Laiah had approached her and has now standing in front of her. Laiah cleared her throat, gaining Latissa's attention.

"If you're done with whatever you're doing over here, we can go ahead and get this paperwork handled and you can be on your way," Laiah told her.

Something in Laiah's tone bothered Latissa, but she plastered on the fakest smile she could manage and held her tongue. As bad as she wanted to check Laiah, she wanted this job even more. She didn't plan on letting anyone mess up her chances of getting Trae. If she had to throw on a few fake smiles and play friendly with a few bitches, then that's what she planned on doing.

"I'm ready whenever you are, boss lady," Latissa replied with a smile. "Lead the way."

Laiah looked her up and down before turning and walking away without another word. Latissa discreetly rolled her eyes to Laiah's back. She would try to keep her cool long enough to accomplish what she'd set out to do, but this was going to be hard. Probably a hundred times harder once Trish returned. Latissa shook off her nerves and put her game face on.

Chapter 10

It was finally about that time for Trish's mini "vacation" to come to an end and she wasn't looking forward to it. She had really enjoyed these last two weeks. This was one of the first times in a while that she wasn't down in Miami because of something pertaining to business. Taz had decided that she would be staying a little longer. She was completely obsessed with her niece and wasn't quite ready to leave her. Taz didn't want to admit it but she had been missing her brothers as well.

"Are you sure you can't stay a little longer?" Sky pouted.

"Hell, no she can't stay," Laiah spoke through their FaceTime call.

Sky laughed and turned her attention back to her IPad's screen. "And why not?"

"One, because we have the club's reopening coming up and Miss Thang ain't been here to help me get none of this shit together. Two, I'm about two seconds from snatching one of these lil' heifers up around here. And three, because I damn said so." Laiah laughed. "Y'all tricks ain't about to be living it up in Miami without me."

"Yo' behind ain't been doing anything but bossing everybody else around," Trish said calling her out. "And who you about to snatch up?"

"The lies you tell, baby. I've been working my ass off. You know your damn brother is a perfectionist," Laiah said. "But you remember that chick, Honey?"

"Honey? Honey, who?" Trish asked. "I only know of one Honey and I doubt if her irrelevant ass is who you're talking about."

"Too bad her irrelevant ass is exactly who I'm talking about," Laiah said rolling her eyes. "Trac hired the lil' bitch. I swear she's getting on my nerves already. She thinks her ass is slick, but I've already peeped game. Trae the only reason her behind wanted this job so bad."

"Who's Honey?" Sky questioned after the comment about Trae caught her attention.

"A nobody who's always trying to make it seem like she's somebody," Trish answered. "Trae ain't about to give that girl the time of day."

"I don't know about all of that. She sure has been making it her priority to be in that nigga's face every chance she gets," Laiah informed them. "Sis, y'all stubborn behinds need to get a grip and work this shit out, because I'll be damned if I let that lil' hoe become my new sis-in-law. I'm slapping any bitch who even tries. Think it's a game."

Sky laughed to try and mask how she was really feeling. "Lay, Trae is single and a grown ass man. He's free to do what he wants. What he has going on is none of my business," Sky spoke.

"Ugh." Laiah let out in frustration. "T, please hit her ass for me." Trish did exactly that and laughed.

"Don't be hitting me," Sky said. "What y'all expect me to do? Yeah, I still love him, but I guess it just wasn't our time."

"Okay, I'm done talking to you because you're about to make me cuss you out. What you mean, what we expect for you to do?" Laiah fussed. "We expected you to fight for your damn relationship. But nah. You just gon' let him ride off in the sunset with the next bitch."

"Dang, Lay." Trish laughed. "You ain't got to go in on the girl like that."

"Yes, I do," Laiah stated matter-of-factly. "And you can shut up talking to me, too. You and Mills working my last nerve right along with them. All y'all need to get it together before I start knocking heads off."

"Bitch, you on your period or something? You sure are going in on everybody today," Trish said.

"Whatever." Laiah rolled her eyes. "You just hurry your behind up and get home. I'll be getting you from the airport."

"Okay, mama. We're about to head out in a minute anyways," Trish informed her.

"Well, I'll just see you then. Bye, Sky. I'm going to call you a little later," Laiah told her. "Hopefully, I'll be able to come back down there sometime soon."

"I hope so. Now it's just me and Taz," Sky said. "But you know she's been stuck under the baby. She might as well just have one of her own."

"Speaking of babies," Laiah spoke. "Trish, I'm gon' beat your ass when you get here."

"What the hell you talking about?" Trish asked, feigning innocence.

"Don't try to act like you don't know what I'm talking about, trick," Laiah said.

"Hold on. T, you're pregnant?" Sky asked, shocked.

"Ugh! I'm gon' kill Kay's ass!" Trish fumed.

****

The ringing of Trae's phone was annoying the hell out of him. This was about the third time it had rung in the past five minutes. Frustrated, he threw the covers from over him and blindly searched the nightstand next to him until he came across his phone.

"What, man?" he barked into the phone.

"Get yo' ass up, nigga," Ty said, disregarding his attitude. "Why the hell you still sleep anyway?"

"Because, motherfucker. That's usually what people are doing this early in the morning." Trae sat up, throwing his legs over the side of the bed. "What you want?"

"We may have a problem on our hands," Ty informed him.

"What type of problem, man?"

"Your moms," Ty said simply.

"Quit fuckin' playing with me, Tyree. I'm not going to tell you again," Trae seethed.

"Well, Brenda's ass is about to be a problem. She's already starting with the shit and she ain't even out yet."

"I don't want to hear shit about her. If she wants to come at us, then she can. I'm not showing her ass no mercy. So, if that's all you called to tell me, I got more important shit to do," Trae said.

"Lil' nigga, don't be trying to handle me. Don't forget I'm the oldest," Ty reminded him. "I know she cooking up some and it's only a matter of time before shit hits the fan. I'm not going back down this road with her and I damn sure ain't about to go back to jail behind her ass."

"Why you always got to throw that shit out there? Bitch, everybody knows you the oldest." Trae laughed. "But for real, Ty. Don't let that crazy bitch get in your head. We'll deal with that when the time comes. For now, fuck her and she better stay away if she knows what's good for her."

"You're right." Ty sighed before changing the subject. "You know T on her way back home, right? I think her flight boarded about an hour ago. Lay's supposed to be picking her up."

"Yeah, I talked to her last night. She's still not feeling my ass right now."

"You damn right. She'll kill you behind Sky. You know they stick together." Ty chuckled. "Wait until she gets back. She really gon' be on you."

"Oh, well. She better get over that shit." Trae wasn't worried about Trish and her attitude. "But, let me hit you back. I got another call coming through."

Trae ended his call with Ty and tried to catch his other line before the caller hung up the phone.

"Yo," Trae answered.

"Hey."

"Who's this?" Trae questioned, not recognizing the voice on the line.

"Dang, you forgot me already? I met you the other day. Remember, you helped me with my car?"

"Oh, yeah. Phoenix, right? What's up, lil' mama? How you get my number?" Trae asked cautiously. "I know for a fact that I didn't give it to you."

"I called my phone when you let me use yours," Phoenix answered. "I hope that wasn't too forward of me."

"You good. If you wanted my number all you had to do was ask though," Trae told her. "But what's up?"

"Nothing, I just wanted to thank you again and thought maybe I could treat you to lunch or something," she suggested.

"Lunch, huh? I guess that's cool," Trae told her. "But let me get back to you though. I got some things I need to handle, but I'll hit you up so we can set something up."

"That's fine with me," Phoenix answered, trying to hide her excitement. "I'll be waiting for your call."

****

Pissed wasn't the word to describe what Mills was feeling at the moment. Once again, he was forced to be in Porsha's presence. He had been trying to do right and be there for anything involving the baby, but she had been taking things a little overboard.

Over the past two weeks, he had lost count of how many times she had called him claiming something was wrong or doing little petty stuff to get him to come around. The only reason she got a pass today was because she had been complaining about having frequent Braxton Hicks contractions and Mills wanted to be sure everything was good. This baby had really been doing a number on her, but lucky for her she was nearing her due date.

"Are you going to sit there frowning the entire time?" Porsha asked with an attitude.

"Don't worry about me and my face," Mills snapped, pulling into the clinic's parking lot.

"I'm just saying. You could at least pretend you want to be here," she said, becoming emotional.

"Porsha, I'm telling you now, don't start that crying shit. Let's go so we can get this over with," Mills said cutting off the car and getting out.

Porsha sat in the car, watching him through the front window. She folded her arms across her chest and stared him down. Mills had already made it to the clinic's entrance and was waiting on her to get out of the car and join him.

"Man, get your ass out of the car, Porsha," Mills fussed. "I hope you ain't waiting on me to open the door."

"You so damn rude. I swear," Porsha snapped as she got out of the car and slammed his door. "I'm big as hell from carrying your big-headed baby and you can't even help me out the car."

"Don't be slamming my damn door," Mills said as he opened the clinic's door for them to enter.

There was a good amount of people in the waiting room, but it wasn't as crowded as Mills had thought it would be, and for that he was thankful. It was bad enough that she was out telling the world that the child was his. The sooner all of this was over, the better.

While Porsha went to the nurses' station to sign in, he found an area ducked off in the corner and took a seat. Porsha finished what she was doing and waddled her way over to him. He shook his head at her. True enough she was big, but she was being too extra with the way that she was walking. It was almost comical.

Mills continued to take in her appearance. He could admit that she wasn't a bad looking chick, but both her hoodrat attitude and the way she carried herself were major turn-offs. If she had any sense, she could maybe find a decent man and quit hopping from dick to dick. Just the thought had Mills heated all over again.

"Why you still got your face all screwed up?" Porsha questioned as she took a seat next to him.

"I thought I told you not to worry about my face," Mills said rudely.

"Why do you have to be like that all the time?" she asked, rolling her neck. "You act like it kills you to be around me now, but it was no problem when we were fucking!"

"Chill out and lower your voice," Mills said coolly.

"Whatever, Mills. I won't say shit else to you." Huffing, she turned slightly in her seat so that her back was to him.

If she thought that he was going to feel some type of way about her little tantrum, she was wrong. He was glad that she had this so-called attitude, because she hadn't said a single word to him during the fifteen minutes or so that had just passed by. If they could just make if through the rest of the day like that it would be perfect.

However, that thought was short lived when she swung around towards him and hit him in the arm. He quickly looked up from the magazine he was reading and stared her down. It took everything in him not the yolk her up in that doctor's office.

"What the fuck is your problem, girl?" he fussed.

"Either that bitch stalking us or your trifling ass got both of us pregnant! What type of mess is that?" Porsha was now drawing attention their way.

"I'm not going to tell you again to lower your damn voice, ole' slow ass girl," Mills fussed. "What the hell you even talking about?"

Mills followed Porsha's eyes with his own and almost pissed himself at the sight before him. Trish and Laiah were standing towards the nurses' station looking in his direction. Right about now he was praying that the floor beneath him would open and swallow him. His luck couldn't have possibly been this bad.

If looks could kill, he would have already died a thousand deaths. Mills had to admit that the look Trish was sending his way had him a little shook. She was the very last person who he would have expected to see here. He wasn't even aware that she had returned home. Right now that wasn't important, though. What he needed to know was how she found out that he would be there with Porsha.

He had to think fast, because the last thing they needed was Trish to act a fool in this damn place. Mills stood from his seat and headed in Trish and Laiah's direction. For some reason, Porsha hopped her behind up and followed right behind him.

"What y'all doing here?" Mills asked as soon as he was close enough to them. "How you even know I was here?"

"Boy, please. Nobody's worried about y'all pathetic asses," Trish snapped, mugging them both.

"You must be if you can't seem to stay away from us," Porsha sassed from behind Mills.

"I don't think anybody was even talking to you, boo. Put that shit on mute and go find you some business," Laiah said to Porsha.

"He is my business." Porsha stepped closer to Mills.

"Mills get your lil' pet before she gets hurt," Laiah warned just as a nurse stepped through the door they were all blocking.

"Trish Martez," the nurse called.

"That's me," Trish said and grabbed Lalah's hand so they could follow the nurse.

"Yo, why the hell is she calling you to the back?" Mills asked, slightly raising his voice.

"It's obvious why they're calling her to the back. Ain't this a clinic for expecting mothers?" Porsha rolled her eyes at Mills. "Use your head, nigga."

Mills ignored her comment and took a step in Trish's direction. "Why is she calling you to the back, T?"

"That ain't none of your business, Preston. Go tend to your baby mama," Trish said tossing her hand in Porsha's direction.

"Boo, don't get cute. Obviously, you in the same boat as I am, *baby mama*." Porsha smirked.

"Now, didn't I just tell you to find you some business?" Laiah was about to head towards Porsha.

"Nah, Lay. Just chill," Trish told her.

Mills focus still hadn't left Trish. Everything was starting to make sense to him now. The constant mood swings she'd started having and not to mention all that random throwing up she was doing in Miami.

"Are you pregnant, Trish?" Mills could feel his anger surfacing.

"I don't have time for this mess." Trish waved him off.

"You better not be pregnant with my seed and ain't said a damn thing to me about it," Mills fussed.

"I don't know what you're getting yourself all worked up for," Trish said folding her arms across her chest. "It ain't like this will be an issue for much longer."

"Fuck that supposed the mean?" Mills barked out. The smirk on her face told him everything he needed to know.

Before anyone could stop him, he was lunging in her direction. Good thing for her she was able to get out of his reach in time. Nurses could be heard in the background yelling for security, but none of that mattered to him. At that moment, all he wanted to do was strangle Trish. The security, along with two other men that had been waiting in the lobby, tried their best to restrain him.

"I put it on everything I love! If you even think about killing my fucking baby, you're dead to me! I'll fuckin' kill you!" Mills yelled as they struggled to pull him from the building.

"Ma'am, you really need to come to the back until they get a handle on this," one of the nurses instructed Trish. "We've already called the police."

"No, none of that's necessary," Trish told them. "I really just want to leave. Can I reschedule?"

"Of course," the nurse told her. "But I really think you should give it a moment before leaving. Make sure he's no longer on the premises."

Trish agreed just so that it could get them out of her face. She couldn't believe that Mills had really just shown his ass like that. Well, yes she could. She knew exactly what type of reaction her little comment was going to get from him. Now she had some shit on her hands that she wasn't ready to deal with.

Chapter 11

"Bo, I put it on my life, if she gets rid of my baby I'm gon' kill her ass," Mills vowed as he paced the floor of his living room.

"Just chill for a second, man." Bo had been trying to calm him down for the past thirty minutes, but nothing seemed to be working. "What the hell even happened?"

"I had to take Porsha's ass to her appointment this morning, right. While we sitting there her dumb ass start going off about how I ain't shit for getting two females pregnant at the same time. So, you know I'm like what fuck you talking about. I look up and T and Lay there mugging the fuck out our ass."

"I swear you have the worst luck ever, nigga." Bo laughed.

"Shut up and let me finish," Mills told him. "You already know T ain't wrapped too tight, so I'm thinking she followed us there or some shit. The nurse come out calling her ass to the back. So, I'm like why the hell they calling you, Trish? Man, I flipped the fuck out. She gon' have the nerve to say it ain't no point in getting all worked up because she wouldn't be pregnant for long."

"Shit." Bo wasn't expecting to hear that.

"It took about everybody in that bitch to keep me off her ass," he said releasing a frustrated breath. "They put my ass out. Then, I had that bitch Porsha in my ear fussing the whole ride home."

"What I want to know is what you call them over here for?" Bo questioned. "You know how those niggas are, especially Trae's hostile ass. He been on one since that shit with Sky."

"Because I'm tired of this shit. I'm telling them straight up that I'm killing T if she gets rid of my seed," Mills said like it was that simple.

"Nigga you buggin'. You should have waited until you calmed down and thought this shit through," Bo said shaking his head. "This gon' get ugly."

"Fuck that," Mills snapped. "It is what it is, but I'm telling them. I'm not about to keep playing games with Trish."

Mills wasn't trying the hear anything that Bo was saying. He didn't want to think rationally right now. All logic went out the window the moment Trish opened her mouth to say that she was getting rid of his baby. He didn't care what they had going on; his baby was innocent and had nothing to do with their beef.

The beeping of the alarm system brought Mills out of his daze and he looked up to find Trae, Ty, and Noc entering the living room. They all greeted Bo first, being that he was standing closer to the entrance.

"What's up?" Trae questioned while meeting Mills fist with his. "What you call us over here for and why the hell you looking like you ready to kill some damn body?"

"Because that nigga is," Bo mumbled.

"What's good, Mills?" Noc asked. "Some shit need to be handled?"

"Nah, man. Nothing like that." Mills sighed, scratching his head.

"Then what?" Trae's impatient ass asked. "You know I don't like playing this damn guessing game."

"Bruh, listen," Mills said trying to find the right words to say next. He had to tread lightly because he knew what he was about to tell them wasn't about to go over easy with them.

"What, man?" Ty asked. "Got a nigga anxious as hell."

"Okay, it's like this," Mills began. "T and I have been fooling around for a good lil minute now and shit's pretty heavy between us."

The room had become so quiet that you could probably hear a mouse piss on cotton. Both Trae and Ty's expressions remained blank as they stared at him. Mills wasn't sure what they were thinking right now because their faces gave nothing away, but their silence was killing him. Bo and Noc both stood to the side waiting for what was about to happen next.

"Look, I know—" Mills tried to get out before Ty rocked the shit out of him.

The blow caught him off guard, but before Mills could get his bearing, Trae followed through with a mean uppercut that landed him on his ass. He couldn't do anything but take it because he knew he deserved that and more. Luckily, he got hit with their fists instead of bullets. Trae and Ty both extended a hand to help him up from the floor. When he was back on his feet, he moved his jaw around trying to readjust it.

"Damn, what y'all trying to do? Break my shit?" Mills fussed.

"Nigga, stop crying." Trae laughed. "What the fuck took you so long to say something?"

"What the fuck you mean?" Mills continued to stroke his aching jaw.

"Exactly what I said. What took you so long? Did you really think we ain't already know this shit? Come on, man. You know better than that," Trae said.

"T butt begged me not to say anything to y'all until she was ready, which I know would have probably been never," Mills told them. "But her ass ain't got a choice now."

Trae just laughed and shook his head. He could tell from the look on Mills face that Trish was giving him hell. Trae thought the entire thing was funny. He didn't really understand why they felt the need to hide things between them for so long anyway. Yeah, he could admit that he and Ty were difficult and hard to deal with when it come to her decisions about her personal life, but this was different. Trae trusted Mills with his life and he was confident that he could trust him with Trish's as well.

"So, T's the one that's been having you walking around here mad at the world?" Noc chuckled.

"Hell yeah." Bo instigated. "Sis taking his ass down through there."

"I hope you ain't finally tell us, thinking that we was gon' help you with her ass." Trae laughed. "Whatever y'all got going on is not our business unless it needs to be."

"You got to deal with her spoil behind, now. That's all you, bruh," Ty told him, laughing as well.

"Y'all laughing at this shit now, but y'all damn sister about to make me strangle her ass. On some real shit," Mills said plopping down on the couch. "Man, T's pregnant and she talking about killing my fucking seed, yo."

"So, not only were you sneaking around with our sister behind our backs, but your ugly ass went and got her pregnant, too? What type of shit is that?" Ty asked. "I should shoot your ass."

"Forget all that," Trae said waving his hand. "What you mean she's talking about getting rid of it? When did you find all this out?"

"This morning, man. Long story short, I took Porsha to her appointment this morning, saw T there and found out we're expecting a baby that she claims she's not keeping, shit hit the fan, and I got put out," Mills quickly explained. "I'm telling y'all now. If she gets rid of my child, she's dead to me."

****

"I thought he was just fixing the damage, not revamping the whole dang club," Trish said as she took in the new appearance of the club.

"Trick, I told you I've been working like a slave around here," Laiah joked. "Trae's difficult ass just had to go adding stuff."

Trish laughed right along with her. She should have known that Trae was going to try and go bigger and better for the reopening. The layout was pretty much the same, but with a few changes. The new addition to the Exclusive VIP room was made of partially frosted glass and overlooked the rest of the club.

Seeing that the dancers he usually had spread throughout the club were so popular, he decided to add an area dedicated strictly for strippers. Initially, his plan was to open a strip club anyways, but this was the next best thing.

The idea was to find some of the baddest strippers around, have then work exclusively at his spot, and offer limited access to them. Easy money. Niggas loved to flaunt, so they were really about to be spending bread.

"Man, this right here is hot," Trish said, as she stepped onto one of the stages and grabbing ahold to the pole placed there. "Definitely a good move. I can see these niggas going crazy now. Spending all they rent and child support money."

"Hey, I didn't mean to cut into y'all conversation," Latissa spoke, interrupting them. "Has Trae made it in yet?"

"What do you need with Trae now, Latissa?" Laiah questioned. "Every two seconds you're somewhere asking where he is. If it's something you need, I'm sure Dee don't mind helping. She is the one I assigned to train you."

"Well, Dee obviously can't help me with all of my questions," Latissa sassed. "Which is why I was looking for Trae."

"Nah, then you should have come to the ones over you, which are us," Laiah said motioning between herself and Trish.

"I really doubt if we would have been any help with the questions she has." Trish smirked. "What? You want to ask how big his dick is? Or if he'll let you suck it? Because those are about the only things we can't help you out with."

"Bitch, I—" Latissa hissed before she was cut off.

"Y'all good over here?" Trae questioned as he approached them.

"Yeah, were good over here. Just straightening out one of your confused employees. Seems like she's having a difficult time understanding how things work around here," Trish informed him before she turned back to face Latissa. "You can get back to what you were doing."

Latissa rolled her eyes and huffed, before storming away. Trish shook her head and turned her attention back to Trae. She hadn't paid any attention at first, but behind Trae stood a pretty caramel-complexion woman who was standing a little too close for Trish's liking.

"Who do we have here?" Trish asked, motioning behind Trae.

Phoenix moved to the side of Trae and extended her hand in Trish's direction. "Hi, I'm Phoenix."

STILL THUGGIN'

It took a moment for Trish to finally shake her hand. From the way Phoenix was dressed, it was obvious that she wasn't there for an interview. Trish didn't want to come off as rude, but she needed to know what Trae was doing with this chick.

"Phe, these are my sisters Trish and Laiah," Trae introduced.

"*Phe?*" Trish questioned before she could catch herself.

"Nice to meet you, Phoenix," Laiah interjected. "But excuse us for a minute. We need to speak with our brother."

Trish grabbed his arm and dragged him away so that they could all speak in private. Trae already knew that it was going to be a problem when Trish and Laiah saw him with Phoenix, but he really didn't care.

"What the hell she doing here? So, this the bullshit you're doing now?" Trish asked with her hands folded across her chest.

"Don't start that shit with me, T. She's here because I brought her here. I'm going to tell you this once. Don't start no shit," Trae warned.

"What about Sky? You willing to just throw everything away like it's nothing?" Laiah asked.

"Man, fuck Skylar! I ain't throw shit away. She did," Trae said, becoming upset. "Look, that's dead and I'm done with this conversation. I got shit to do."

Trae walked away before either of them could get another word out. They both stood with shocked expressions on their faces as they watched him grab a confused Phoenix's hand and exit the club. The mere mention of Sky's name had him so upset that he couldn't think straight.

Phoenix wasn't sure what that was about back inside the club, but she instantly picked up on the change in Trae's demeanor. Not to mention the scowl that was plastered across his handsome face. She reached across the center console of the car and gently placed her hand atop his.

"Is there something wrong?" Phoenix asked, concerned.

"Nah, everything's good," Trae snapped.

"Umm, okay. Trae, we can grab something to eat some other time if you're in a sour mood now," Phoenix suggested.

Trae instantly felt bad about the way he had just snapped at her. He could tell by her tone that she was genuinely concerned.

"No, ma. I told you we were going to grab something to eat and that's what we're going to do," Trae told her. "I apologize about coming at you like that."

"We're good, Trae. Let's just enjoy the rest of our day."

The sweet smile that adorned Phoenix's face brought a calm over him. She was a really cool chick to hang out with. They had been together since earlier that afternoon and it surprised Trae how well he could vibe with her. She may not have been Sky, but she would do for now.

Chapter 12

"You sure you're ready?" Stacey questioned Sky as their plane was approaching the airstrip.

"It's a little too late to be trying to second guess now," Sky answered with her game face on. "Just ready to get this over with."

There had been a meeting called with the heads of the top families once word got out that Santiago Empire was about to be back in the forefront. A lot of people were shocked and still in disbelief after hearing that Ace was indeed back.

"Siah and them got in earlier to make sure everything's set. Everybody else should already be there waiting for us," Stacey informed Sky.

Sky just nodded her head and listened as the pilot came over the intercom informing them that they had made it to their destination. As soon as Sky stepped off the plane, she noticed a man in an all-black tux standing next to a cocaine white Rolls Royce Phantom. Sky remembered the last time she had rode in one of them. It was her eighteenth birthday and her dad and Stacey had gone all out for her. She had been chauffeured around the entire day in one.

The entire ride Sky sat quietly taking in the scenery. It had been so long since she got to visit that she forgot how beautiful of a country Colombia was. Sky was so lost in her trip down memory lane that she didn't realize that they had reached their destination. Something about the place seemed quite familiar to her. After further examination of the exterior architecture, she realized that it had a lot of the same details as the estate back in Miami.

"Okay, baby girl," Stacey said grabbing her attention. "You're about to be in the presence of a lot of powerful people. But I want you to remember one thing; you're just as powerful. You don't even have to open your mouth when we get in here if you don't want to. The fact that you're present at this meeting already says enough."

Sky nodded her head as she took in everything that Stacey was saying. Instead of being nervous like she thought she would, she was calm. The adrenaline that was rushing through her at that moment pushed out all fear and hesitation that she had been feeling on the plane. Her game face was in place and she was ready for whatever awaited her inside. Stacey had of way of bringing the beast out of her that she thought had long ago died.

Stacey looked down to check the notification that had just come through his phone. "Showtime, baby."

This was it. As they walked through the halls of the huge residence, Sky knew that there was no going back. This meeting was about to change everything. She was on an entirely different playing field now and this wasn't kiddie shit here. They were in the big leagues.

As she and Stacey entered the room, everyone stood to acknowledge their arrival. There were only six people present at the round table when they entered. All men. They all greeted Stacey with manly hugs and their customary kiss on the cheek but seemed hesitant about Sky.

"*Hijo*," Don Jairo said pulling Stacey into his arms. "*Ha sido tanto tiempo.* Too long. Glad to see you're in good health."

"I know and I'm glad, too," Stacey said pulling out one of the chairs for Sky to take her seat.

"Listen, Ace. I know you've been out of the swing of things for quite some time, but nothing's changed," Don Fernando spoke. "Your little arm piece will need to wait outside until this meeting is adjourned. *Lo siento, cariño.*"

"Well, considering the fact that this little *arm piece* is running the Santiago Empire, I think you gentleman can make an exception," Sky spoke calmly.

"What?" Don Fernando asked incredulously. "What is she talking about?"

"Come on. I know you're not hard of hearing. So, from here on out, watch what comes out of your mouth. Your status means nothing to me," Stacey said taking his seat next to Sky. "Is this going to be a problem for any of you? If so, you might want to speak up now."

Don Hernan leaned forward in his chair and reached for Sky's hand. She was a bit hesitant at first but considering the fact that Stacey hadn't made a move she just went with it. When he brought her hand to his lips, she relaxed a little.

"*Bienvenida, Hermosa*," Don Hernan greeted. "It's an honor to finally meet you. Please excuse the confusion and accept this apology on behalf of all of us."

"Let's just move forward," Sky said accepting his apology.

"There are very important introductions that need to be made, but I'll keep things short," Don Jairo spoke.

He went around the table and introduced each man, stating which family they were head of. Something about Don Fernando rubbed her the wrong way. She would be sure to speak with Stacey about it once they were alone.

Don Jairo motioned with a wave of his hand and seconds later they all were brought a flute filled with champagne.

"Gentlemen," Don Jairo said grabbing everyone's attention. "Don Stacey. Don Skylar."

That one simple acknowledgment had just changed everything. Once Don Jairo raised his glass, everyone else followed suit and raised theirs.

"This has been a long time coming, Don Stacey," Don Hernan acknowledged. "All of your late father's territory is in both of your hands."

"With no issues, correct?" Stacey glanced at Skylar before focusing his attention back on the men.

"The heads of the families are all in agreement. There are no issues," Don Jairo assured him, but his focus had briefly moved to Don Fernando. "But your situation with Santana needs to be handle as soon as possible. He's bad for business and we don't have time for the attention he's been bringing the organization."

"No need to worry about that. It's as good as handled," Stacey told them.

****

"You motherfuckers must have made some sort of pact and decided you were all going to show your ass," Kay fussed. "Is that what the hell going on?"

"Calm all that mess down, Kayla. I ain't even did shit this time." Bo sighed.

"This time? There should be no times! I'm so damn tired of y'all shit."

Kay continued to fuss as she stood in the kitchen fixing breakfast. Mills and Noc had just gotten there a little while ago and she had been going in on Mills since he stepped foot in the door.

"Only one that seems to have some sense and know how to act is Noc's unstable ass. You don't see him running through women or putting them through all this unnecessary bullshit," Kay said slamming a plate down in front of Bo and Mills.

"Because his ass gay." Bo laughed.

"Fuck you, pussy-boy," Noc said accepting his plate from Kay

"Baby, why am I getting fussed at for shit that Mills and Trae got going on? I ain't been on shit but trying to make sure those niggas ain't out here going on a damn killing spree." Bo stuffed his face with food. "You need to be on this nigga right here."

"Oh, it's like that?" Mills asked.

"Hell yeah. I ain't about to be in the doghouse because of your ass."

"That's T ass with the games. Not me. Ain't shit going on with me and that damn girl other than her possibly about to have my baby. That's it. Trish's stubborn ass don't want to listen though, so it is what it is. I'm not about to kiss her ass. But one thing I do know is that she better not get rid of my child."

"If I'm correct, which I know I am, you and Trish were already kicking it when that baby was conceived. She's pissed off and hormonal right now, Mills and you can't really blame her. You know she wouldn't do no mess like that," Kay tried to reason.

"I don't know shit. All I know is what came out of her mouth." Mills could sense himself about to get upset all over again.

"Yo, we got to be out. Trae just texted me 911. Something went down at the spot in Kirkwood," Noc said getting up from his seat and going to place a kiss on Kay's temple. "Thanks for breakfast, sis."

"Don't be putting your crusty ass lips on my woman," Bo fussed.

"Shut up and bring yo' ass, nigga," Noc laughed.

Not too long after, they were all pulling up to the stash house in Kirkwood. Trae's car was already there, but it didn't surprise them that he had beat them there. They unloaded and headed inside to see what was going on. Things had been pretty quiet since their return, so they weren't sure what this was about.

"What the hell happened in here?" Mills asked, taking in his surroundings.

They entire place had been completely trashed. All the furniture had been destroyed. There were huge holes in a majority of the walls and same of the floorboards had been ripped up. Whoever did this was damn sure determined to find whatever they were looking for.

"That bitch," Ty bellowed.

"Who?" Noc asked.

"Brenda's stupid ass," he answered.

"Shit," Bo cursed.

"Wait. Your moms? That Brenda? I thought that psycho was still locked up," Mills said.

"She is, but she'll be getting released real soon and the bitch been sending threats every damn day," Trae fussed. "She's lucky I'm not able to get to her right now or she wouldn't be breathing."

"But what makes you think she got that much pull to be coming at y'all from the inside? This could be that nigga Slim's doing. They never did find that nigga."

"I'm pretty fucking sure," Trae said motioning behind him to one of the walls they overlooked.

Someone had used bright red spray paint to write "Brenda's Back" in big, bold letters. Even though this was a serious situation, shit was still kind of funny. Brenda had it out for you kids ever since their father Tyree Sr. was granted sole custody of them.

Tyree Sr., or "Big Ty" as the streets called him, did everything is his power to make sure Brenda was happy and wanted for nothing. Whatever she asked for, she got. That still wasn't enough for her. She loved the thrill of being able to stand next to her man and bust her guns with him. She loved being able to ride shotgun while he was making plays and handling business. All of that was ceased when they started their family and he put an end to that, which she wasn't too pleased about.

She slowed down once she had Ty and Trae, but that didn't last long. Brenda hated the whole domesticated housewife routine and her old habits quickly began to resurface. She was back to the constant partying and had really slacked off on her duties as a wife and mother. If it hadn't been for her accidentally getting pregnant with Trish, things between her and Tyree Sr. would have ended way before it did.

The final straw was when he found out that she had been stealing from him and using his drugs for years. Brenda tried to blame her drug use on being so stressed out by the children and not being able to handle all the responsibilities thrown at her.

That confession made his next move a lot easier. He didn't hesitate at all to put her out of their home and file for divorce, along with seeking full custody. Ever since then, Brenda had made it her duty to make their lives a living hell and she had been doing a pretty damn good job at it.

Trae refused to let her continue to have a hold on them. He was ready to end this and put this behind them. He and his siblings had been through enough because of her and he wasn't about to let her continue to ruin their lives.

Chapter 13

It was nine in the morning and Trish was sitting in the waiting room of her new doctor's office waiting to be seen. After everything that went down the last time, she no longer wanted to go back to the other clinic, so she had them recommend her another obstetrician. Besides, she wouldn't dare show her face in that place again after the scene Mills caused.

Trish still haven't gotten confirmation on how far along she was, and she was anxious to find out. That bit of information would help her make her decision on what to do about the baby. It didn't help that she didn't have anyone that she felt like she could talk to without them judging her. Taz and Kay had already made it perfectly clear where they stood. Sky wouldn't be much help either because she already had a lot on her plate. Laiah didn't offer much of an opinion and was there to support her through whatever.

Times like these had her wishing she could go to her brothers, but that thought went out the window just as quickly as it came. It was killing her to keep this from them. Especially now that things had gotten really crazy. Her brothers would wait until she had the baby and kill both her and Mills. She laughed at the thought.

"What's so funny?"

Trish froze as soon as she heard his voice. She just knew she had to be tripping. When she finally looked up to find the source, she dropped her head right back down.

"Nah, ain't no point in that," Trae said taking a seat next to her.

"Trae, what are you doing here?" Trish asked.

"Nah, I should be asking you that."

"Umm. I was umm... I," Trish stuttered trying to come up with an excuse.

"Before you answer, be sure that whatever's about to come out of your mouth is the truth," Trae told her.

By the tone is his voice and the expression on his face, Trish could tell that he already knew the truth. She was busted.

"Why didn't I find this out from you?" Trae asked. "T-Baby, since when do we keep secrets from each other? You know we don't even operate like that."

"I know and I'm sorry. You know how you and Ty are though and honestly I was afraid of how y'all were going to react."

"Baby, don't ever be afraid to come to me. I know you don't have the sanest brothers." Trae laughed. "But never feel like you can't come to us. Mills is our boy and as much as I want to put a bullet in that nigga for even going there with you, I know I have nothing to worry about with him."

"I wouldn't be so sure about all of that," Trish mumbled.

"Listen, what y'all have going on really ain't my business, but I will say one thing. Don't always assume shit. Take the time out to listen to what that man has to say. I know you, T. You probably ain't even had not one conversation with him and swear you know what's going on."

"So, you're taking his side? That's not fair, Trae," Trish whined.

"I'm not taking his side, but it's not like I know your side of things since you're going around hiding shit. All I'm saying is sit down with Mills and actually talk. This ain't about just y'all anymore, so something needs to be figured out before my niece or nephew gets here."

Their conversation was brought to a halt as the nurse came out and called Trish to the back. Trae was right behind her. After Trish had gotten changed and situated in the examination room, Trae entered and took a seat in the corner.

"You nervous?" Trae asked.

"A little," she admitted. "All of this is new."

There was a knock at the door before the doctor entered the room. Dr. Mathews introduced herself to both Trish and Trae before directing her attention to Trish. Trae couldn't help but check out the doctor's appearance. Her clothes didn't reveal much, but Trae could tell that she was working with a nice little body under that lab coat. The smooth chocolate skin that adorned her petite body had Trae nodding his head in appreciation.

Once Dr. Mathews started with the exam, Trae was thankful that he had chosen to sit off in the corner. He wasn't interested in seeing all his sister's business. If he would have known all of this was about to go down, he would have opted to stay in the waiting room.

"Alright, you guys," Dr. Mathews said standing and going to wash her hands. She placed a new pair of gloves on her hands and went back over to Trish. "Come on, big brother. I'm going to do an ultrasound so that you guys can hear the baby's heartbeat."

Other than the swooshing sounds coming from the machine, the room was silent as they waited. After a few seconds of prodding around on Trish's stomach with the ultrasound wand, they finally heard it.

"Oh my God." Trish hand flew to cover her mouth. "That's my baby? Listen, Trae."

Trae chuckled at her excitement. "Yeah, I hear it, T. Damn. My baby about to have a baby on me. I don't think I'm ready for this."

Dr. Mathews laughed. "She's ten weeks along, so it looks like you have a enough time to get ready."

After cleaning Trish up, she was able to get dressed. Both Trae and the doctor had stepped out to give her some privacy. Now that she was left alone with her racing thoughts, her feelings were all over the place. After hearing her baby's heartbeat for the first time, there was no way that she could see herself getting rid of her child. There was already a connection. Whether she liked it or not, she knew that she needed to sit down and have a talk with Mills. After all, they were about to be parents.

****

Trish sat in her car dreading going inside the warehouse. She should have known that Trae wasn't about to let her off the hook so easily. After they finished with her checkup and counseling session, he let her have it. A part of her knew that she was the one in fault for this entire situation. She had been doing everything to push Mills away and used the situation with Porsha as a scapegoat.

The truth of the matter was that she was afraid. She was afraid of him actually loving her. She was afraid of a relationship between them working. Never had she been with someone long enough to really consider a future with them. In the past, she only occupied her time with people who she knew she saw no future with. Trish was afraid of allowing herself to be vulnerable with someone, because she feared they would use that against her and take advantage.

There were only a handful of people that she trusted enough to open herself up to and those people were her family and her crew, which is partly why she found herself in the predicament she was in now. Trish trusted Mills with her life. No, he wasn't perfect, but she could bet her life that he would never do anything to intentionally hurt her.

A knock at her car window startled her and brought her from her thoughts. She turned to see Mills standing there with a blank expression on his face. The look on his face almost made her second guess her decision to come there. It probably would have been better to catch up with him some place public where there were witnesses in case he tried to kill her ass. They hadn't seen or spoken to each other since the disaster at the doctor's office.

"You plan on just sitting out here staring at the building all day?" Mills finally spoke.

She let out a nervous chuckle before shutting off the car and getting out. He didn't say anything else. Instead, he turned and headed back inside with her following behind him.

"What you doing here?" Mills asked, getting straight to the point.

"Umm. We need to talk," she told him.

"Talk?" Mills questioned with a pissed off chuckle. "When I wanted to talk you weren't trying to hear shit I had to say. Since you got something to say, now all of a sudden we need to talk? Nah, ain't shit for us to talk about. Unless you're about to explain to me how the hell you just gon' up and kill my fucking seed!"

"If you would just shut the hell up and listen! Damn," Trish yelled.

"Who you talking to, Trish? Don't make me strangle yo' lil' ass in here. I'm already trying my best not to lay hands on you behind that shit and that ain't even me," Mills fussed.

Trish let out a frustrated breath and massaged her temple. She had to get a handle on this conversation if they were going to make any progress. She took a moment to collect her thoughts before she spoke again.

"Look, Preston. I didn't come here to argue with you. Okay," Trish said in a calmer tone. "First off, let me go ahead and put it out there that I didn't kill your damn baby, so you can stop with the threats. And sec—"

Before she could finish what she was saying, Mills had grabbed her and pulled her tightly into his chest. What felt like hours passed before he finally released her. His eyes searched her face to be sure that she was telling the truth. He had been really messed up in the head since she had told him she didn't plan on keeping their child.

Out of all the women he'd been with in the past, he could never picture himself actually having offspring with them. Even the situation with Porsha hadn't fully registered yet. Kids weren't really something he saw for himself, but that changed the moment he realized that Trish was pregnant with his child.

That moment changed everything. He could now see himself being someone's father. Hell, even someone's husband, but he didn't want all of that with just anyone. He wanted it with her. That moment was ruined though. Ruined by the possibility of it all being snatched away from him.

"Please don't be playing with me right now," Mills begged. "So, we're having the baby? You're keeping it?"

"Why would I even play around about something like that? Yes, we are definitely having a baby," Trish confirmed.

Mills picked her up in his arms and spent her around. His celebration didn't last long before she was fussing at him to put her down. The moment her feet touched the floor she took off for the restroom. If there was one thing she hated about this pregnancy, it was the ransom nausea.

"I'm sorry about that," Mills said, handing her a damp paper towel once she was finished. "You don't know how happy you just made me, man. You about to bless a nigga with his first child!"

"Second," Trish corrected. "Don't forget Porsha's baby."

"The verdict's still out on that one. Don't ruin the moment. Let's get out of here and go grab something to eat. We still got a lot to talk about."

"Can we go to Wing Factory? I've been craving their hot wings," Trish said, already envisioning what she wanted.

"Nope. You ain't about to be feeding my baby no damn hot wings," Mills fussed.

"Please don't start this already." Trish shook her head as they left out of the building. "Your car or mines?"

"Yours. I rode up here with Noc," he said while opening the car door for her. "Let's get it. You driving, baby mama."

"Don't call me that mess."

"Be quiet, mean ass, or I'll change my mind about feeding you," Mills joked.

"And you'll be right on the side of the road. You know not to play with me about my food." Trish laughed. "Especially not now."

MEL G

Mills just laughed and shook his head. He was glad that they could be in the same space without going at each other's necks. Things weren't going to change overnight, and it was going to take some more work, but at least they were headed in the right direction.

Chapter 14

"I'm leaving out later tonight," Taz told Sky as they both were sifting through the racks of clothing. "You know the reopening's tomorrow, right? I think you should come."

Taz had spent all morning trying to convince Sky to go back with her to Atlanta for a few days. Sky was already missing everyone else and was tempted to take Taz up on her offer. The only thing stopping her was Trae. Trish had informed her already that he had been spending quite a bit of time with a new woman and that broke her heart.

As much as that hurt Sky to hear, she couldn't really blame anyone but herself. A man like Trae was not about to sit around pining over her for too long. It was time for her to come to terms with the fact that things were really other between them.

"Earth to Skylar," Taz called, waving her hand in Sky's face. "I know you heard me, chick."

"Yeah, I heard you, so stop being so extra." Sky laughed. "You know me going is not a good idea. And besides, Stace and I have business to handle."

"Whatever. You get a pass this time. Come on so we can check out. I'm supposed to be having dinner with Von and Mar before my flight."

"Cool. I'm getting tired anyway and I need to be seeing about eating something myself," Sky said heading towards the register.

Taz looked at Sky and checked her out. "You keep eating the way you do and that lil' thick ass of yours ain't gon' fit in them jeans you're carrying. They been over there stuffing you."

Sky nervously chuckled. She had noticed how quickly she was beginning to gain her weight back. During to time that she was being held by Jayceon and Slim, she had lost almost a good twenty pounds. The only thing they really allowed her to eat was soup and crackers and that was just to be sure that she didn't die on them from starvation.

Now, she had gained that weight back plus some and it was getting harder and harder to hide her growing baby bump. Stacey and Dr. Baranov had been on her about getting to a healthy weight for her and the baby's safety. She was already high risk and was doing everything she could to ensure a safe and healthy pregnancy, but she may have been going a little overboard in the food department. It seemed like she was hungry even two seconds. She was almost eating just as much as Stacey and the triplets, which was an extremely hard task to accomplish.

"I couldn't be walking around here looking all anorexic and stuff. I'm small enough as it is," Sky joked.

"Well, that weight looks good on you," Taz complimented her and they left out of the store.

Julio wasn't too far behind them. With Santana and Slim still out there lurking around, Sky wasn't able to step foot out of the house without someone with her. Julio walked up and took their bags from their hands as they all proceeded to the truck. After dropping Taz off at Von's house, Julio made sure to stop and pick Sky up something to eat before taking it in.

"You ready to see Dr. B?" Julio questioned with a cheesy smile on his face.

Today Sky had an appointment with Dr. Baranov to hopefully find out the sex of the baby. It seemed as though this pregnancy was flying by. Granted she had not too long ago found out, but she was still in disbelief that she was in her second trimester already. She couldn't wait for the day she finally got to meet her little angel. Stacey and her cousins were just as bad as she was. If they weren't discussing business, then it was all about the baby.

Their excitement warmed her heart. She found herself often wondering would Trae be just as excited. Every time she thought about their situation, she found herself getting sad. Not telling him about the baby was wrong and she knew it. The problems they had now were nothing compared to the ones they were about to experience once he found out.

"Are you okay over there, Sky Boogie?"

"Yeah, Ju. I'm fine. Just ready to find out whether I have a little mister or misses swimming around in here," Sky answered, rubbing her belly.

"How long you plan on keeping this a secret? I don't know if you've noticed, but baby girl you're getting bigger by the second."

"I don't know. I haven't had the chance to think things all the way through," Sky answered.

"Well, you might want to get to thinking. If it wasn't for the fact that you've been wearing all these huge clothes, I'm sure your girl would have noticed by now. Unless she's just not saying anything because that shit ain't hard to miss."

They pulled up the long driveway and stopped in front of the entrance. Before they could even get the car in park good, Stacey was stepping outside and approaching the passenger door.

"What took y'all so long? Dr. B's already here and has everything set up," Stacey informed them while helping Sky from the car. "I'm trying to make sure everything's good with my nephew."

"Nephew? Nah, it's a girl in there," Julio stated.

"Bet money it's a boy," Stacey challenged.

Sky stood there and shook her head at the two. This had been a continuous debate around the house. It didn't make her any difference though. As long as her baby was healthy, she would be okay with whatever the gender turned out to be.

"Half a mil says it's a girl," Julio said.

"Y'all cannot be serious right now," Sky said before walking off to leave them there.

"About time," Josiah said when she entered through the door. "Stop slow poking around so we can see what we're having."

"Ughhhh. Not you too, Siah." Sky sighed. "Y'all are so annoying. If I didn't know any better, I would think that this was y'all baby instead of mine."

Stacey threw his arm around her shoulder and led her to where the doctor was waiting. "Stop all your whining. You're the first of us to have a kid, so this is all our baby. Stop trying to hog him to yourself. You might as well suck it up because you have to deal with our annoying assess for a very long time."

"Ms. Skylar," Dr. Baranov called out as he approached her with open arms.

Over the past couple of weeks, she had really grown the love the old man. His spirit was so sweet that it often had her wondering how on Earth he came to work for her crazy family.

"How have you been since we last met? Have you been following my instructions?" he questioned with a scowl on his face.

Sky couldn't help but laugh. She hadn't been the easiest patient and her hard-headed antics had her being constantly scolded by the doctor.

"Yes, Dr. B." She chuckled. "I've been following your instructions to the T."

"Good to hear. Now let's get started. You know these four are a real impatient bunch," Dr. Baranov joked.

Things were looking pretty good so far. Just like she had suspected, Sky had gained back all the weight she lost plus some.

140

Those forty pounds seemed to have found their way straight to her ass and hips.

"Considering the condition you were in when you first arrived, the weight's good. It's still a little under where I would like for you to be at this point in your pregnancy, but you're progressing well," the doctor told her. "Now for the fun part. Time to check this little critter out."

Stacey and her cousins all huddled around Sky while the doctor powered on his machine and prepared to start her ultrasound. Sky giggled once the cool gel touched her stomach. She still hadn't gotten used to that. With her attention now on the screen, she tried to see if she could make what the images where in front of her.

Sky took notice to the weird look that was on Dr. Baranov's face. He was concentrating hard on whatever was on the screen. Every few seconds he would press a few bottoms and then scratch his head with a weird look on his face.

"Is something wrong, Doc?" Stacey asked with a worried expression on his face.

"Oh no. I assure you nothing's wrong. I'm just trying to figure out how I could have possibly missed this," the doctor answered.

"Missed what? What's going on?"

Sky could feel herself beginning to panic. If nothing was wrong like he said it was, then why was he asking so strange? Sky needed answers now before she lost it. Stacey sensed her uneasiness and began to run his hands through her hair. That was something that he had been doing since they were kids to help sooth her and he was thankful that it still worked.

"Calm down, Ms. Skylar. There's no need to get yourself worked up," the doctor assured her. "I'm just not sure how I missed an entire baby. He was doing a pretty good job of hiding."

"What are you talking about?" Sky asked, confused. "And wait. Did you just say he?"

"Whoo! What I tell you, O? Didn't I say it was going to be a boy?" Stacey gloated as he slapped hands with Jonas. "Need to be hitting that safe don't you, playboy?"

"Man, forget you."

"Mr. Stacey you might not want to celebrate too soon," Dr. Baranov said.

"And why not? He owes me half a mil."

"Well considering the fact that she's caring twins, both boy and girl, I don't think that bet is still valid," Dr. Baranov announced with a smirk.

"Twins! What do you mean twins?" Sky shrieked, jumping to an upright position. "That can't be right, Doc. You may want to check again. *Please* check again."

"Ms. Skylar I'll check again only for your peace of mind, but I'm pretty sure there's two little jokers occupying that there stomach of yours."

"Ughhhh. This janky family! Twins really? We're cursed man," Sky fussed.

"What you trying to say?" Jonas laughed.

"Look on the bright side, Sky Boogie. You got a two for one special," Julio joked and quickly dodged out of the way when she moved the swing at him.

"Don't be trying to put all that on our side. Trae's folks have it just as bad. Hell, even his pops was a twin."

"Huh? I never knew that," Sky said shocked.

****

"Damn," Laiah exclaimed over the loud music. "We definitely did the damn thing."

"Man, what! This shit turned out hotter than the first opening. Thanks for coming through, Lay. You know I couldn't have pulled this shit off without you," Trae congratulated.

"Well excuse me then," Trish said. "I guess I don't get any credit."

"Nope. You sure as hell don't because while you were too busy playing around in Miami, Laiah was here busting her ass," Trae said. "I appreciate what you do, T, but Laiah gets the credit for this one."

"Let's continue to enjoy the night, you guys," Laiah spoke.

Trae agreed and hugged his sister before raising the bottle of D'ussé in his hand and saluting her. Trish decided to let his comment go simply because she knew he felt some type of way about her choosing to stay back with Sky instead of returning with them.

"Hi, Trae," a voice spoke from behind them.

Trish turned first and instantly felt the urge to roll her eyes at the sight of Phoenix. She seemed like a really okay person and hadn't done anything to raise any red flags so far, but Trish just didn't think that she was the one for her brother. She honestly didn't have anything against her other than the fact that she wasn't Sky.

"What's up, Phe? Damn, you looking good, girl. I didn't know you were coming, but I'm glad you made it," Trae said extending one of his arms out to hug her. "Even though you're late as hell."

"Sorry about that. It took me forever to get in here. That line almost made me change my mind and turn around."

"You should have told me that you planned on coming and I would have just put you on the list. You remember my sisters Trish and Laiah, right?"

"Of course. It's nice to see y'all again," Phoenix said politely.

"Yeah, you too," Laiah returned with a forced smile.

An extremely familiar face moving through the crowd caught Trish's attention, causing her to hit Trae's arm a little harder than intended. She couldn't help it though.

"T, please don't start with your mess. I'm not trying to hear any of that," Trae said, shutting her down before she even thought to say something about Phoenix being there.

"Look towards the main bar," Trish instructed.

Trae followed her instructions and his jaw tightened the moment his eyes landed on the person that Trish pointed out. They had some nerve showing their face in his club. Trae knew that there had to be something up to this random appearance after all these years.

"Yo, where's Ty? I need y'all to find him and keep him wherever the hell he's at until I get this motherfucker out of here," Trae ordered.

Laiah did what he said and rushed off in search of her man. She didn't know the entire story behind the beef between all of them, but she knew enough to know that Ty needed to be kept as far away as possible. Instead of going with Laiah, Trish decided to follow Trae. Before they made it to the bar, their intended target turned around to face them. He began clapping loudly as the duo approached him, bringing attention to all of them.

"Trae. Look at you. This is quite the establishment you have here. Your father would be so proud of you."

"Don't speak on my father," Trae gritted out. "What the fuck are you doing here?"

"Whoa, is that any way to talk to your family? I mean I am your uncle." His uncle Tyrell smirked, his face housing identical features to their late father.

"You're no family of ours and I suggest you leave while you still have the choice."

Tyrell laughed, but not a laugh of humor. This was stemmed from anger. "I'm not family? Lil' nigga whether you like it or not, I'll always be y'all family. Shit, you look like I could have spit your ass out my damn self. All y'all motherfuckers do!"

"Are you done yet? I got more pressing shit to tend to," Trae said as calmly as he could.

"So, you're big shit now, huh? I remember when your pissy behind was running around with your head tucked so far up your brother's ass. Now, all of a sudden, you're the big man in charge," Tyrell taunted.

Trae couldn't respond even if he wanted to. Before anyone knew what was going on, Ty had pushed his way through the crowd and pounced on their uncle. No words left his mouth, but the look in his eyes said it all. Murder was the only thing on Ty's mind at that moment.

"Chill! Yo, Ty! Let him go, man!" Trae yelled. "Now is not the time! You trying to go back for the same shit!"

Trae and a few members of his security team had finally managed to get Ty away from their uncle, whose face was bloody and almost unrecognizable. Trae instructed his team to escort him out and to not let him back on the premises. He had to get him as far away from Ty as he could because he knew that Ty wouldn't hesitate to kill him. Now was not the time for that. There were way too many witnesses around and it seemed as though everyone had focused their attention on them.

"Aye, round up the ladies and get them out of here," Trae instructed Mills and Bo. "Noc, can you keep an eye on this nigga? I need to make sure everything's good before I bounce. I'll be right behind y'all."

Trae knew that his staff would have no problems closing up without him being there. Right now, he needed to figure out why his uncle had decided to appear out of thin air. With everything else that had been going on this was too much of a coincidence to ignore. He needed answers, and he knew exactly where to find them.

Chapter 15

Sky confidently strolled through the hotel's entrance with both Julio and Jonas flanking her sides. Their appearance alone screamed power and money. It was as if everyone could sense there status just from their presence. Or maybe it was the fact that her cousins stood next to her built like two huge statues, surely intimidating anyone whose path they crossed. They both held hard expressions on their faces that were far from welcoming. That wasn't why they were there. Their job was to protect. To be her muscle.

"Good evening, ma'am. Welcome to the Hyatt Hotel. How may I be of assistance to you?"

"I have a reservation under Santiago," Sky told the woman.

"Oh yes, Ms. Santiago. We've been expecting you and I've handled your requests personally. I hope everything meets your standards. Enjoy your stay. Please don't hesitate to let me know if there's anything else I can do for you."

"Thank you, Indigo," Sky said reading her name from her badge. "I shouldn't be needing anything else. You have a nice day."

Once they had everything squared away, the first thing Sky did was take a nice relaxing bubble bath, followed by a quick cat-nap. That flight had really drained her. After she awakened, she felt rejuvenated and ready to handle business, but first she had to put something on her stomach.

"I'm about to order something to eat. I'm starving," Jonas said going through the hotel's menu.

"You must have read my mind. Get me a big fruit salad. Make sure it's fresh" Sky requested as she headed into the living area. "Oh, and see if you can get me some crab legs, too."

"That's some combination." Julio chuckled.

After the food had arrived, they all sat around discussing the meeting that was to take place in a few hours. Sky wasn't worried about going into this deal without Stacey. This was the reason why Stacey had given her the position in the first place. He was confident that she would be able to handle things on her own. Though she appreciated his belief in her, she still had a lot to prove to herself.

"We have a little time before you're scheduled to meet with this guy. I want to get there early and scope things out to make sure shit's solid," Jonas said.

"That sounds good to me. I'm about to get dressed and then we can head out." Sky stood.

"Cool, I'm about to check in with Stacey," Julio said pulling his phone from his pocket.

Sky excused herself and moved to the room she was occupying so that she could get ready. Her wardrobe had changed significantly since she assumed the position as one of the leaders of a well-known crime family. She was a boss and was expected to present herself as such. So it was out with most of her old things and in with new. Even though she enjoyed shopping to pass time, that task was no longer necessary. Now she had personal shoppers who did all of that for her and delivered all type of goodies to her doorstep.

One of her favorite looks that they had gotten her was a fitted Crépe tuxedo jacket with matching bottoms from Ralph Lauren. Sky had fallen in love with the ensemble the moment she tried it on and knew that the look would be perfect for this meeting. She topped off her look with a pair of Veau Valors Louboutin pumps and her red clutch. If she wasn't sure about anything else, she was positive that she looked damn good.

"Let's get it, Boogie," Julio called from the other side of the door.

Sky emerged from the room and smoothed her hand over her bottoms. "Let's get it."

It didn't take them long to get to their destination because Stacey was sure to pick a hotel that was in somewhat close proximity. They all took in their surroundings. The area was a pretty upscale one, but there was nothing too spectacular about the building itself. It was pretty bland and unwelcoming and had Sky wondering if they were in the right place. The valet and bouncer standing guard told her that they were.

"What can I do for y'all?" the burly doorman asked.

"Mr. Mason is expecting us."

Sky stood erect with her head high. Her eyes were hidden behind huge Chanel frames, guarding her expression.

"Wait here." The doorman disappeared inside.

It didn't take long before he returned and granted them access. To say that Sky was shocked once they entered would be an understatement. The outside definitely didn't do the inside justice. The space was elegantly decorated with accents of silver throughout, but the darkness of the place added an air of mystery.

"Mr. Mason wasn't expecting you all so soon. Please make yourselves comfortable and he'll be with you shortly," the man instructed and then excused himself to resume his position at the door.

They were approached by a server within a few minutes of sitting down. This girl was walking seduction and screamed sex appeal. Sky almost got lost staring at her before Julio snapped her out of it and asked her what she would like.

"Cranberry juice is fine," Sky answered.

"Coming right up, beautiful," the server said and walked away.

"They definitely have a nice selection of women working in here."

"With the clientele they bring in I would hope that the quality of girls is up to par. Everything's top of the line. You have to have a Black Card to even get into this place," Jonas told them.

They were approached by two men, one of which was the owner, Gerald Mason. Sky had done her research ahead of time and knew all there was to know about Mr. Mason here.

"I see you all made it here Welcome to 'What's Yours?' I'm Gerald Mason, the owner."

"What's your *what*? That name leaves a lot to the imagination," Sky pointed out.

"What's your fantasy? Fetish? Fear? Desire? Here we strive to answer all of those," he answered while approaching Skylar. "Our goal is to know it all, beautiful."

"I see," Sky said simply.

Gerald winked at Sky and stepped away. He turned his attention to Julio and Jonas. "I'm assuming you two are Ace and Duece, right?"

"Actually—"

"Excuse us for a moment, beautiful. This boring business stuff shouldn't take too long, so help herself to anything you'd like while us men handle a little business," the man that was with Gerald finally spoke.

"I'm sorry, but I didn't catch your name," Sky said, removing her glasses and turning her attention to him.

"Nigel Vann."

"Okay, Nigel. Maybe I should introduce myself." She extended her hand out to him. "Hello, I'm *Deuce*."

Sky smirked at the shocked expressions on both Nigel and Gerald's faces. Surely, they hadn't expected that.

"Those two behind me are Grim and Reaper. Are there any other introductions that need to be made or can we get started with this meeting?" Sky questioned with a raised brow.

"Umm... No, there's umm... We're good here," Gerald stuttered. "Just a surprise, but no problems. You all can follow me to my office."

Julio noticed the nasty look that Nigel shot Sky's way before heading in what they assumed was the direction of Gerald's office. Gerald motioned for everyone to sit, but Julio and Josiah declined and opted to stand. They both stood on guard behind the chair that Sky occupied and kept their expressions blank.

They weren't there to converse. Once again, they only had one focus—to protect Sky and have her back if she needed them. Everything else pertaining to this meeting was irrelevant to them.

"Okay, so we were thinking that it would be a great investment to expand and Miami is high on our list. Something like what we have here would do major numbers down there. The projected market isn't as upscale as it is here in New York, but there's still big money."

"I'm quite aware of that. All the discussed terms are still the same. Sixty off top will go to us, not including whatever additional debts you acquire on the miscellaneous end of things," Sky said, referencing the drugs.

"That's correct, and we still agree to those terms," Gerald told her.

"Excuse me, Gerald. Nigel, is there a problem? You seemed to have a scowl affixed to your face and I'm curious as to why," Sky spoke.

"I assure you there's no problem, Deuce," Gerald quickly spoke before cutting his eyes at Nigel.

"Why are we discussing business with you when Ace is the one we set all of this up with? If he's who we were expecting, then he's who should have shown up. I don't know how you all do business, but we have a certain way we go about things around here and sending one of his little pregnant girlfriends in to close a major deal ain't one of them," Nigel spat.

"Nigel," Gerald bellowed out.

"What? You act like we can't do this without them. Why are we even doing this in the first place when they're trying to take sixty percent of profit? We don't need them!"

"Quiet, Nigel! Why are you trying to fuck this up?" Gerald asked angrily. "I apologize for my partner's behavior, Ms. Deuce."

"No need." Sky slid her shades back over her face. "You have until midnight to come to a decision, because it doesn't seem as though you and your partner are on the same page. You have six hours."

She stood to shake Gerald's hand before she signaled to Julio and Jonas that they were leaving. As she passed Nigel, she heard him mumble "bitch" under his breath. Stopping, she leaned down close to his ear.

"Just know that this *bitch* is about to become your worst nightmare."

Sky placed a kiss on his cheek and stood back to her full length. She sauntered over to the door where Julio and Jonas stood awaiting her.

"What was that about?" Julio questioned.

"I want him," Sky said discreetly. "I'm sure we have a few places here, so find the closest one and have him there before midnight. I don't care how. Just make it happen."

Jonas shook his head and laughed. Sky was in rare form today and she wasn't holding any punches. If Nigel were a smart man, he would have kept his mouth closed and let his partner do all of the talking. Since he wasn't, he now was about to pay for that slip of the tongue. Not with money, but with his life.

****

"Ahhh! Fucking bitch! Let me go!"

"There goes that bitch word again," Sky taunted, standing in front of Nigel's dangling body.

Just as she'd requested, Julio and Jonas had snatched Nigel up with no problem and had plenty of time to spare. One of the perks of being so powerful was having access to almost everything you could think of. Property being one of them. All it took was one phone call and Sky had the perfect location to carry out her plans for the night. The building they were in was about an hour from the city and pretty much secluded.

Nigel sat, or more like swung, in front of her with a mixture of sweat and blood running down his face. He had a nasty gash on his head which resulted from all of the struggling he did after Sky instructed her cousins to strip him down.

"If you're going to kill me you might as well get that shit over with! I'd rather die before I beg a bitch like you for anything!"

"Nigel, you really should work on that filthy mouth of yours. I would think that someone of your stature would be more poised," Sky said.

"What's going on here? What's this?" Sky heard from behind her.

"I'm glad you could join us, Gerald. Come join Nigel and me over here," Sky beckoned.

Gerald hesitated to move, causing Jonas to shove him in Sky's direction. "You heard her. Move."

Gerald slowly approached where Sky stood, not sure of what was about to happen next. He noticed the belt in Sky's hand and figured that must have been the cause of the numerous welts on Nigel's bare torso.

"See, Gerald. I've done a little research on your partner here. This guy's a real shady character." Sky laughed.

When Gerald didn't say anything, she continued talking. "Your partner's been doing a lot of deals behind your back. A lot of deals that won't need you. Isn't that right, Nigel?"

"Suck my dick," he barked.

Julio stalked up and delivered a crippling blow to his gut. "Speak to her in that manner again and I'm going to cut your tongue out and shove it down your throat."

"Fuck you," Nigel spat and hocked up as much saliva as he could before spitting the bloody mixture in Julio's direction.

Sky motioned for Julio to stand down but kept her attention on Gerald. "Did you really think I would agree to a deal that involved this disrespectful motherfucker? That's a little insulting. No worries, though. I'm about to give him a crash course in manners."

Jonas walked over and handing Sky a bag carrying the items she had requested. Her eyes lit up like a kid in the candy store once she unzipped it and revealed the contents.

"You seem to always need to be reminded of the extra load you're carrying," Jonas scolded. "Deuce, don't overdo it or I'm damn sure telling Ace."

"I know my limits," Sky assured him.

"You better hope so because I'm not trying to hear his damn mouth about why we let you go through with this shit in the first place."

Sky turned to Gerald. "You know that deal we agreed upon earlier? Well, that's no longer on the table. From now on, Nigel's out and instead of sixty, we'll take seventy-five."

Gerald let out a defeated sigh. "Do I have much of a choice?"

"Unfortunately for you, no. But you can thank your so-called partner for that," Sky said. "But look on the bright side. At least you still have your life. Too bad that after the night's over with, Nigel over there won't be able to say the same."

****

Trish sat on Mill's sofa with her legs propped up on his lap, trying to focus on their conversation and the foot massage she was receiving. That was proving to be extremely difficult with the constant ringing of his phone.

"I want you and the baby here with me, T. I don't really see a point in you going out and getting your own spot. I've got plenty of room here and I would feel comfortable with my child close," Mills said.

"I need time to think about that. That's a really big step. If we're going to do this, we need to do it right. I don't want to go through this whole back and forth thing," Trish said.

"Well, I'm in this and I'm willing to work on us, but I want us to be on the same page, too. If you need time to think about it then I guess I have to be cool with that."

His phone began to go off again. Trish finally got fed up with hearing it and snatched it up from where it rested on the coffee table.

"Either answer and see what the hell she wants or block her. I'm tired of that damn phone ringing every two seconds. Literally every two seconds! Damn," Trish fussed and snatched her legs from their comfortable position on his lap.

"Calm that mess down, T. I'll handle it."

"You better before I do it for you," she sassed.

"What man? Why you blowing my phone up?" Mills barked into the phone.

"Don't be yelling at me! If you answered the first time, I wouldn't have to blow you up, now would I? You let that bitch make you forget that you have responsibilities? Really, Mills?" Porsha yelled into his ear.

"Watch that disrespectful shit that's flying out yo' mouth right now. What do you want, Porsha? I'm only going to ask once."

"You know I don't have any transportation. I've been trying to get in touch with you because I have things that I need to get in order before the baby gets here," she told him.

"Why you can't call one of your ratchet ass friends? They be quick to give you a ride when it has something to do with some bullshit," Mills said.

"They not the ones who laid down and got me pregnant, nigga! That ain't theie responsibility," she fussed.

"Shut all that shit up! What all you need to do, man?"

Trish sat listening as he went back and forth with Porsha. Stuff like this wasn't going to cut it. She understood that Porsha was supposedly carrying his child as well, but this chick just didn't understand boundaries and couldn't stay in her place. Once Trish heard Mills say that he would be there within the next few hours, she got up from the sofa and headed to his room.

Mills was right behind her after he ended his call and followed her into his bedroom. He watched as she removed his boxers that she had been wearing and replaced them with her jeans. Once she began searching for her shoes, he finally stopped her.

"Baby, what are you doing? Why are you putting your clothes on?"

"What does it look like? I'm about to go," she answered, slipping her feet into her shoes.

"T, you're making a big deal out of this and leaving for nothing. We were doing good. I'm only going over here to take her to get this stuff for the baby and that's it," Mills explained.

"Ain't nobody about to leave your ass, Preston. But I am going with you to the bitch's house, so let's go," Trish said and left him standing there.

The entire ride to Porsha's house Mills begged and pleaded with Trish to be on her best behavior. Both were pregnant so he really hoped that nothing popped off. Between Porsha's flip mouth and Trish's hot temper, he knew that that was only wishful thinking. Hopefully luck would be on his side today, because lord knows it hadn't been any other time.

"I'm not playing, T. Don't go in here flying off the handle and you know you're carrying my child," Mills said as they pulled into Porsha's apartment complex.

"Whatever. As long as she doesn't get out of line with me I won't have to beat her ass and everything will be good."

"Nah, see. I knew I shouldn't have let your ass come. You with that shit, man."

"Nigga, you ain't *let* me do nothing. Now get your ass out the car so we can get this over with. I'm tired, hungry as hell and really not in the mood to be spending my afternoon dealing with your baby mama."

"You should have stayed at the house then," Mills mumbled as he got out of the car.

Trish didn't wait for him to open her door. She hopped right out at the same time he did. "I shouldn't have stayed no damn where. You ain't about to be nowhere near this bitch unless I'm right there, too."

"Bring your lil' behind on and follow me and you better watch how the fuck you talking to me. I let that shit slide enough, but don't forget I will fuck you up out here, T. Try me."

"Whatever," she said rolling her eyes.

Mills didn't care about any of that. He smirked at her and shook his head. She may have had a little attitude, but she knew better than to test him. She shut right on up and followed him the rest of the way to Porsha's apartment door. He knocked hard and waited for her to answer.

"Who is it?"

"Open the door. It's me," Mills announced.

"Why didn't you tell me you were on the way?" Porsha asked as she unlocked and opened the door in nothing but a tiny robe that barely covered her huge stomach or ass. "What's she doing here?"

"Don't worry about what she's doing here. Worry about finding some damn clothes and putting them on. I told you that I would be here sometime in the next few hours, so you should have been ready."

"I don't want her in my house, Mills," Porsha said, ignoring him and still focused on Trish. "I can't believe that you had the audacity to show up at my house with this bitch."

"Watch your mouth, baby girl. I'm not gon' be too many more of those. Pregnant or not, I'll still beat your ass all up and through this little ass apartment," Trish warned.

"I wish you wou—"

"Kill that shit! I ain't in the mood for all this bickering," Mills said shutting them both up with a glare. "T, did we just not have this conversation two seconds ago? Go over there and sit your butt down! And Porsha take your ass in the back like I said and find some damn clothes. I'm not trying to be dealing with you all day."

"Now you can't move on your own without having a chaperone? You know what? Don't even worry about it. I don't need you to take me anywhere. I'll find another damn way." Porsha huffed. "I'm not about to be riding around with y'all like we some damn sisterwives or some shit."

"Baby girl, you need to—" Trish started but Mills cut her off and told her to be quiet and let him handle it.

"If you don't do what the fuck I said and hurry up so we can leave," Mills gritted out. "Don't test me Porsha because the way I'm feeling right now, I could really body your ass and not give a single fuck."

MEL G

Porsha stormed away to her room and slammed the door behind her. Mills ran his hands over his face and through his hair. These women were going to be the death of him. He was sure of it.

Chapter 16

Trae looked around and took in the decor of Heavenly Hands Spa. He had to admit that the place was nicely put together. The soft grey and lavender color scheme really gave the place a tranquil vibe. This was his first time inside of a spa, but had he known they were this relaxing he would have made it his business to visit one a long time ago.

"Good afternoon, sir. What can I help you with?" the bubbly receptionist greeted.

"I'm looking for my friend. She works here," Trae answered. "Phoenix."

"Okay. Let me see if she's free right now," she said reaching for the phone. After a few words with whoever was on the phone, she turned back to Trae.

"She's finishing up with a session right now. It'll probably be about ten to fifteen minutes."

"That's fine. Is it cool if I wait over here?" Trae said motioning to the set of sofas they had placed out front.

164

"That's no problem at all. There's tea and refreshments also. Make yourself comfortable," she offered before getting back to her duties.

Since it seemed as though he would be waiting for a minute, Trae decided to go through the million emails that he had piling up. There were a few important ones that he had been on the lookout for and he wanted to be sure that they didn't get lost amongst all the junk.

"To what do I owe the pleasure of this lovely surprise?" Phoenix asked as she approached him with a huge smile on her face.

Trae stood and greeted her with a hug. "Was just over this way and thought you might be hungry or something."

"I guess it's a good thing you're a mind reader, because I'm starving." She giggled. "Hey, Zora. Do I have any more appointments for today?"

The receptionist searched through the appointment book before answering. "Nope, Mrs. Jenkins rescheduled. So, I guess you're free unless you want to take a few walk-ins."

"No, I think I'll just take the rest of the day. See you tomorrow." Phoenix waved goodbye as she and Trae exited the building.

They had been kicking it pretty heavy the past couple of weeks and Phoenix was really into him. As much as she didn't want to admit it, she knew that Trae was still hung up on his ex. The two never discussed the topic, but Phoenix felt it was time for them to have the conversation. She could really see herself being with him, but she wasn't trying to set herself up for that heartbreak.

"Can I ask you something, Trae?" Phoenix questioned.

They were walking through the mall after grabbing a bite to eat. Since she had the rest of the day off, they figured they would chill and enjoy each other.

"Yeah, what's up?"

"What's the deal with you and your ex?" Phoenix inquired. She noticed the way that his jaw flexed at the mention of his ex. "I'm sorry if I'm being too nosy."

"Nah, you're straight," Trae said. "Nothing's up with us. She's doing her thing and I'm doing mine."

"Trae, listen. I'm really feeling you, but to be honest, I kind of feel like you may be stringing me along."

Trae released a sigh. From the way this conversation started he could tell that it more than likely was about to ruin the mood. "Man, what are you talking about? Where's all this coming from, Phe?"

"Come on. Even a blind person can see that you're still very much in love with Sky and I'm only here to pass time."

"You serious? That's not even true. Why can't I be kicking it with you because I think you cool as hell and enjoy your company?" Trae asked her.

"You still love her?"

Trae thought about her question. He already knew the answer, but he had been trying to convince himself otherwise. Regardless of what he told himself and everybody else, he knew that his feelings weren't going to change.

"Yeah, I still love Sky," he answered truthfully. "But sometimes that isn't enough. We weren't on the same page with certain things. I was ready to go all in but shit just didn't work out."

"Do you don't think that there's a chance that you guys can maybe work things?"

"Honestly, I don't know. Like I said, I was ready for the whole nine with her. Kids. Marriage. All that and those feelings just don't disappear overnight. Who knows? Maybe someday down the line it could happen." Trae shrugged.

"I see."

Phoenix couldn't do anything but respect his honesty. Trae could have easily told her a bunch of crap that he thought she wanted to hear. The fact that he put his cards on the table and kept it real with her had her feeling him even more. That level of honesty seemed hard to come by nowadays.

"Phe, I'm sorry if that's not what you want to hear. I'm feeling you, but I get where you're coming from and I understand that you have to protect your feelings," Trae said. "To be real with you, I can't offer you much right now because that's just not where I'm at."

"It's okay. I understand, Trae."

"I hope that doesn't change anything between us. I told you before that I really enjoy kicking it with you and I meant that. Hopefully, we can maintain a friendship."

"I would really like that." Phoenix smiled.

"So, since we're doing this whole friend thing does that mean I can't feel up on yo' booty no more/'" Trae joked and laughed when she playfully hit him in the chest.

"You're so damn crazy." She giggled.

"I'm dead ass serious. Don't act like you don't be liking that shit. It has to be some perks to this shit."

Phoenix shook her head and was about to give a smart comeback until a pair of shoes on display caught her attention. "Speaking of perks. I think you should be a good best friend and get me these. You can't say these aren't sexy."

"Oh, now I'm best friend?" Trae chuckled. "Boy, you women are a trip. But you're right. Those joints are hot. Go ahead and get them. Just know I'm rubbing all up on that booty later."

Phoenix blushed at Trae and turned to find someone to assist her. Before she could take a step, she was being roughly bumped into. She was caught off guard and stumbled back. If it wasn't for Trae moving to catch her, she would have landed flat on her ass. She looked in the direction of the person responsible.

"My bad. I didn't see you standing there."

"Latissa? What you doing here?" Trae questioned.

"What's up, Trae? Oh, excuse me. It's Mr. Martez, right?" Latissa laughed. "I'm just here doing a little shopping before going to work tonight. I do have a life outside of the club, you know. Who's your friend?"

"This is Phoenix. Phoenix, this is one of the girls who works down at the club, Latissa," Trae introduced.

"Nice meeting you," Phoenix replied.

"Umhmm. Well, let me get out of here. See you later, Trae," Latissa said and walked away.

Trae looked at her strangely as she walked away. There was something up with her. Her vibe seemed off and the way she acted towards Phoenix didn't sit well with him. Trae shrugged her off for the moment and concluded that he would just deal with her later.

****

"So, he's not with that Santiago bitch anymore?" Tyrell questioned.

"I'm guessing not, because now he's been parading around with some new bitch."

"Okay. Shit's probably not that serious with her so she's irrelevant right now. Have you learned anything new? We've given you enough time that you should have something that we can work with."

"Not much. At least not from Trae. He's a hard man to get close to and he shuts me down anytime I even try to get close to him. I think the key is Trish. She and Laiah are always at the club so it shouldn't be a problem getting to her. If you want Trae and Ty to come to you then that's the way to go. I know for a fact that they'll tear this city up looking for her. Shit, snatch Laiah's ass, too."

"You're right." Tyrell nodded.

"Nigga, are you slow? We tried that shit already and you see how that turned out," Slim spoke from the corner.

"No, your incompetent ass tried it and failed miserably. If you would have stuck to the original plan, we wouldn't still be doing this same song and dance. You're the one who fucked up by making a deal with that motherfucker Money that almost cost us everything! Sit your ass over there and let us handle this," Tyrell barked.

"Man, get real! You already know what the fuck you're up against and you're sending this dumb ass broad on a fucking suicide mission! You want to sit here talking shit about me not getting the fucking job done, but I see you over there nursing two ugly ass black eyes and a bruised jaw courtesy of those niggas," Slim fussed.

"Are y'all serious right now?"

"I bet this nigga didn't inform you on the fact that these motherfuckers have killed off every fucking body working with us, which is why he's even wasting time with your ass. He needed somebody dumb enough to agree to this shit," Slim told her.

"Look, I don't know what y'all niggas got going on, but I'm done with this shit. I told you all I know. I'm out. I need to get to work."

"Honey, wait! Latissa," Tyrell called after her.

Slim looked at her and shook his head as she got up to leave. She had no clue what she was getting herself into. Slim regretted the day that he agreed to work with this cat. Tyrell was a joke in Slim's eyes and he surely didn't have what it took to be in charge. He had no idea what he was doing and was way in over his head, but Slim wasn't crazy. Something was telling him that Tyrell wasn't the one calling the shots, which would explain a lot.

"Man, leave her ass out of this shit. You ain't gon' get shit accomplished by trying to take them damn girls. That only gon' put you into some shit that you can't get out of. Think bigger than that petty shit," Slim said.

"Oh, I'm thinking a whole lot bigger. See, what you don't understand is that you have to play dirty with people like them because they're not just going to bow down. You have to make them."

****

Stacey sat at his desk mugging the computer screen. He was beyond pissed off and ready to hop on the next plane. He stared into the camera, listening as Sky explained why she had totally disregarded the entire conversation they'd had prior to her leaving.

"Come on, Stace. You would have handled the situation a million times worse." Sky rolled her eyes.

"It doesn't matter! I can do that shit, you can't," he yelled.

"And why the hell not? How are you going to say that we're equal in this, then the next minute you're yelling at me about what I can and can't do?"

"Don't try to be cute, Skylar. This has nothing to do with that and you know it. This is about the fact that you can't be doing all that shit. I don't care if they were there with you or not."

"You do it, so what's the difference?" Sky questioned stubbornly.

"I'm not the one pregnant," Stacey yelled at her. "If something happens to my niece and nephew, I'm gon' hurt you. I'm not playing with you, Skylar. Chill the fuck out. That's what Julio and Jonas are there for in the first place. Let them do that shit. Your job is to sit back and give orders."

"Yeah okay, Stacey. From now on, I'm let them handle the dirty work. Is that better?" Sky sassed.

"That's what you were supposed to be doing in the first place. I swear you're trying to run my blood pressure up, man. I'll be glad when you stop being difficult and tell Trae, so you can stress his ass out. I'm not trying to go to an early grave worrying about your hard-headed behind."

There was a knock at the office door. Josiah entered and took a seat in the empty chair in front of the desk. He waited and let Trae finish with his video call.

"I got to go, baby girl. I need to talk with Siah," Trae told her. "Remember what I said. I'm not playing."

"Yes, father. Is there anything else, sir?" Sky joked. "Bye Stacey. I'm going to be on my best behavior. Bye Si!"

"Bye, baby girl." Josiah laughed as Sky disconnected the call. "What trouble have those three gotten into already? They've barely been gone a good two weeks."

"I think this pregnancy has turned your cousin into a damn psychopath. She's out here trying to kill everything moving." Stacey chuckled. "I thought O was the wildcard, but she may have him beat. Even he said it."

"That's what you wanted, right? You're not slick, Stacey. You sent her to deal with people who you knew for a fact would be on an ego trip and try her just because she's a female. Looks like she's handling business and I'm sure they're getting the message she's sending loud and clear. Before long they'll know not to fuck with her and not just because she's associated with us. But because they know what she's capable of," Josiah said.

"Exactly." Stacey smiled. "But what's up? What you got for me?"

"Guess who's been seen in our neck of the woods." Josiah smirked. "I've had eyes on your man Don Fernando since the meeting, like you requested. Especially considering the fact that he never usually makes such frequent trips. He's been here few times too many for my liking, so I did a little digging."

"How long has he been here?" Stacey questioned.

"Flew in two days after we did. Been here since, but he's been back and forth between here and Cali. He's been renting out a beach house out there for about two months, way before he got here and conveniently booked the same day we ambushed that safe house," Josiah informed his cousin. "And you'll never guess who the occupant is."

Stacey was pretty sure that he already knew. "Get a private flight ready. We need to leave within the next hour because we have a few stops to make," Stacey told him.

"Trust me. I'm way ahead of you."

"Well, let's go. This needed to be handled like yesterday," Stacey said standing and heading for the door. "I need to call an emergency meeting with the heads. Call them and let Sky know that they need to be leaving out now and meeting us there. See about getting a plane for them," Stacey instructed.

It took them no time to make it to their first stop, which was Medellin, Columbia. There was a specific protocol that needed to be followed first. Stacey couldn't order a hit on the head of a family without calling a meeting with the other heads and getting approval. That was grounds for having your entire family executed. Even then, it wasn't a guarantee that they would agree with your reasoning.

Luckily for both Stacey and Sky, the meeting went in their favor. The other heads were in agreement and had already been aware of his ill feelings towards them and the position they held. Don Fernando was the only one to voice his distaste with the decision to bring them both to the family and everyone else took notice. If he was conspiring to take them down, it wasn't much of a surprise to anyone.

The only thing that was required of them was to be sure that Don Fernando's body was in good condition when they were done, so that it could be sent to his family. That wasn't an issue at all because he wasn't really Stacey's focus. With the amount of pull and power that Stacey and Sky had access to, one would think that they would just hire someone to make this problem go away, but that wasn't good enough for them. Under different circumstances maybe they would have, but this was personal and something they needed to handle on their own.

"I guess our next stop's Cali," Stacey said as they all settled onto their private plane.

****

"Mills," Trish called out, barely awake. "Mills get your phone. Preston, get your butt up and answer that phone!"

"Damn, man! A nigga can't even sleep in peace," he fussed while blindly reaching his hand from under the covers in search of his phone.

Once it was in his reach, he snatched it up but it had already stopped ringing. Just as he was about to put it back it started ringing again.

"Hello," Mills answered groggily.

"Umm, hi. Am I speaking with umm... Mills? This is Porsha's aunt Cheryl."

"Yeah. She straight? Everything okay with the baby?" Mills asked sitting up.

"That's why I was calling. We just made it up here to the hospital. Her water broke a few hours ago and I guess now the contractions are really hitting her," she informed him.

"Okay, what hospital? I'll meet y'all there," Mills said getting up and moving around the room to find something to throw on.

"Is everything okay?" Trish asked from the bed.

"Yeah, Porsha's just in labor. I need to head to the hospital."

"I'm coming," Trish said throwing the covers from over her.

"Alright, come on," he said before turning his attention back to Porsha's aunt on the phone. "I'm on my way. Can you send me her room information and everything?"

"Sure. I'm about to text it to you now."

"I guess it's the moment of truth," Trish said sliding her feet into her UGG boots.

"I guess so."

Mills grabbed her jacket and helped her into it before they left out and headed to the hospital. The entire ride there, Mills was quiet and lost in his thoughts. He knew that he had been adamant about Porsha's baby not being his, but the small chance that it was had started to get to him.

The thing that worried him the most was the fact that he and Trish hadn't discussed what would happen to them if it turned out that he was indeed the father. They had made so much progress and Mills felt that all that could possibly be about to go down the drain.

"You ready? Looking a lil' nervous over there," Trish said from the passenger seat.

"I'm good, baby. Are you ready?"

"More than ready. We'd better hurry up before we miss everything." Trish laughed.

Mills followed the directions that Porsha's aunt had sent him, and he was thankful that they got in with no problems. As they approached the room that Porsha was in Mills stopped and turned to Trish. Trish's face was full of confusion as she searched his for answers.

"T, I need to know that regardless of what happens that it won't affect us and what we have. I need to know that you're in this and not going to walk away if it turns out that this baby is actually mines," Mills said with pleading eyes.

"Preston, come on. You picked a fine time to be trying to have a heart-to-heart," Trish said about to move around him, but he stopped her.

"I'm serious right now. This shit will either make or break us. Promise that you'll ride it out with me."

"I'm here, ain't I?"

"That ain't good enough for me, baby."

"I'm not going anywhere, Mills. I knew the moment that I agreed to work this out that there was still a chance of this being your baby. I understand that if it is, that child will a big part of our lives and I accept that. Now if that's all, can we take our behinds in this room?"

Mills smiled and grabbed her hand, pulling her towards the door with him. He knocked before opening the door and entering. Porsha was lying back against the hospital bed with sweat beading down her forehead. Her hair was all over the place and sticking to her face. She looked like she had been going through it.

Porsha turned her attention to the door and frowned once she saw them standing there. Once again Mills had the bright idea to bring Trish along with him, not considering the problems that it would cause. Porsha rolled her eyes in their direction before pulling herself to a seated position.

"Was it necessary for you to bring her?" Porsha asked.

"Yeah, it was actually. Please don't start with this, Porsha," Mills said.

"I'm just saying. I laid down with you, not her, so why does she have to be involved with everything?" Porsha fussed.

"Porsha, let's go ahead and get a few things straight. If this is my baby, I'm going to be a part of her life without a doubt. What you need to realize is that Trish isn't going anywhere. She's a part of my life which means that she will be in this child's life as well. You can make this hard or you can be a grown woman about it and stop with the bullshit. That's on you," Mills told her.

"Whatever, Mills. I'm not about to deal with this right now," Porsha said right before another contraction hit her. "Ahhh! Oh my God!"

"Just breathe through it like they showed you," her aunt coached while dabbing her forehead with a cool rag.

"I'm going to wait down in the lounge," Trish informed Mills.

"You sure? Trish we can leave if you want. She'll just have to call me once the baby's here."

"No, baby. I'm not about to let you do that. What if this is your baby? I can't be the reason that you miss your daughter's birth. I don't want that on my conscience. Stay Preston. We're good. Just come get me once the baby gets here," Trish said and placed a quick kiss on his lips.

Mills grabbed Trish and pulled her back before she could get away and kissed her lips again. "I love you, T."

This was the first time that Mills had told her he loved her and it caught her off guard. "Umm. I... I love you too, Preston."

This time when she moved to leave, he let her. Now he needed to focus on Porsha, who looked like she was about to pass out at any moment. He approached the bed and passed her the cup of ice chips that she was trying to reach for. She looked at him skeptically and mumbled thank you.

Her aunt informed him that the doctor had not too long ago left from checking on her and things were still progressing at a snail's pace. Mills decided to chill in the recliner that was seated by the window next to her bed and sent a text to Trish to update her. Hours had passed, and he had tried to talk her into going back to his place but she refused.

"Knock, knock. How are we doing in here, mama?" the doctor asked as he entered the room.

"I'm not sure. I'm feeling a lot of pressure down there," Porsha told him.

"Alright. Let me take a look."

Mills stepped out of the way as the doctor went over and washed his hands before putting on a pair of gloves. He walked over and lifted the bottom half of the sheet that was covering Porsha's legs.

"Oh, wow. You're crowning," the doctor announced before giving instructions to his assisting nurses. "Looks like we're about to have a baby folks!"

Chapter 17

"How long will it take to disarm the security system?" Stacey asked Jonas as he watched him in the backseat.

"Give me five," Jonas answered, focused on the computer screen in front of him.

"Cool. Alright, Siah. Y'all wait for the word and we only have ten to get in and out," Stacey told him. "Okay, Sky. You're with Jonas. Don't move without the okay. All I need for you to do is take out the two out front. If you're as good as you say you are, you can do that shit from the van."

"Don't play with me, Stace. I can make this shot in my sleep. Just hurry up so we can get this over with," Sky said, shooing him away.

Stacey laughed before going to take his position. It didn't take long before Jonas had completed his task. The moment he gave Sky the signal, she positioned her .308 sniper rifle with the suppressor at the window and aimed at her first target. It took her no time to take them out.

"Showtime," Jonas said before addressing his brothers through their earpieces. "System's down. Y'all boys need to move in now. In and out. Make it clean."

In a matter of minutes, Julio was giving them the signal to bring the van around. Two bodies were tossed in the back before they all climbed inside.

"For a motherfucker of his status, this nigga real lax with his security," Stacey said referring to Don Fernando. "Let's roll."

****

Brenda stepped outside of the gates and took in a deep breath of fresh air. Finally, after fifteen long, agonizing years she was a free woman. It felt good to be on the opposite side of that gate and made a promise to herself to never come back to that place.

She looked through the crowd of people awaiting their loved ones until she spotted her ride. Once she did, she threw the small bag of possessions she had over her shoulder and headed in their direction.

"Look, who they let out. I think the streets are about to be in trouble." Tyrell laughed as he greeted her.

Still after all these years, looking into his face managed to make her feel some type of way. A chill ran down her spine as she looked into the eyes of the man almost identical to her late ex-husband's. The only difference between the two was the fact that while Tyrell was a bit on the slim side, Big Ty was exactly what his name said.

Standing at 6'5 and weighing a good two-hundred and eighty pounds of muscle, Tyrell Sr. was a pretty large man. That's what had attracted Brenda to him in the first place. That and the fact that his entire being screamed power, which was something that Tyrell always wanted. He didn't have the heart for this business. He figured that since his brother was big, that would automatically give him power and respect as well.

Boy was he wrong. True enough, he got a lot of passes off the simple fact that he was Big Ty's brother. That was probably the only reason he hadn't been offed a long time ago. The reputation he had in the streets wasn't a good one. A lot of people wanted him dead and after Big Ty washed his hands of him that gave all those people the greenlight they needed. That only fueled Tyrell's hate for his brother.

"It's good to see that you're on time," Brenda said bypassing him and walking straight to his car.

Tyrell shook his head and went to get into the car so that they could leave. They had a long ride ahead of them and he used that time to update Brenda on everything that had been going on. She was not pleased to hear that after all this time they still hadn't made any progress. It's not like she thought that going after her children would be a simple task, but damn. She could have made more progress than this on her own.

"So, what you're telling me is that you're no closer than you were the last time? What the fuck do I need you for if you can't even do your job?" Brenda barked.

"Brenda, chill with that shit. You knew just like I did that this shit wasn't going to be easy."

Tyrell killed the engine as they pulled up to his home. Brenda turned her nose up and looked over his place in disgust. He pinched the bridge of his nose and counted down in his head to keep from going off on her. Instead of saying anything else, he got out of the car and didn't wait to see if she was following.

The house might not have been the fanciest but at least he could say it was his. Brenda walked in and took in his place. She was fresh out and didn't even have a pot to piss in, but she wanted to act as though she was too good to be in his home. Tyrell watched as she walked over to Slim who was laid out on his couch.

"Is this what y'all been doing? Nigga sleeping like he ain't got shit he needs to be doing," Brenda bellowed as she kicked the couch hard.

"Yo! What the fuck, man? Fuck is your problem?" Slim yelled as he hopped up from where he was laying.

"Ain't it something that you could be doing other than sitting around on your ass?"

"Aye, Tyrell. Who the fuck is this bitch? You need to be getting her the fuck out of my face," Slim yelled.

"Who am I, huh? I'll show you who I am," Brenda said and snatched up the gun from the table, which she assumed was his.

"Whoa. Brenda chill," Tyrell said from behind her.

"You ain't about to do shit with that but piss me off. Now I advise you to pu—"

STILL THUGGIN'

His sentence didn't make it all the way out before she was sending a bullet flying through the center of his skull. Blood splattered everywhere before his body crashed to the floor.

"Are you fucking serious? Why the fuck would you shoot that man? And you got blood all over my shit!"

"Shut the fuck up and clean this shit up! We got shit to do and y'all niggas around here playing," she said stepping over Slim's body and pulling out a cigarette.

She searched through her pockets for a lighter but came up empty handed. "Got a light?"

Tyrell shook his head and stood staring at her in disbelief. His ignored her and moved to find something to clean and dispose of this body with.

****

"How you feeling about everything?" Trae asked as he and Trish sat on the couch in his living room.

This was the first place she thought to come the moment she got the news. Her emotions were all over and she needed a moment to regroup. For some reason, talking to Trae always seemed to help her see things clearly. Things had been a little strained between the two of them since the return from Miami, but Trish had to admit that she missed the way things used to be.

For some reason she and Trae had always shared an extremely close bond. It had been that way since they were younger. Yeah she was close with Ty, but it was different.

"Honestly, I really don't know how I feel, Trae. I know I said that I would stick it out, but that was before. Is it wrong of me to be mad that she's actually his daughter? I know it's not right, but I can't help how I feel."

"T-Baby, you have every right to feel that way. But I will say one thing. You made the choice to stay when you could have walked away," Trae reminded her. "If you feel like you can't move past this and know you're probably going to still hold this over his head, then you need to walk away."

"I don't want to walk away. This is just going to take me a minute to digest. The baby's not really the issue because she didn't ask to be here. It's the mother. You know Porsha and you know she's going to try to make our lives a living hell."

"Don't give her that type of power. Y'all need to all sit down and have a talk, because like it or not y'all kids are about to be siblings," Trae preached.

"Oh, we gon talk alright. She ain't pregnant no more," Trish said.

"But your ass is! T, don't make me fuck you up," Trae fussed.

"I'm not about to risk my baby for her ass. I may be pregnant, but my girls aren't. She can get out of line if she wants to and she'll have a nice ass whooping waiting."

STILL THUGGIN'

Tho doorbell sounded off throughout the house and Trae got up to answer the door. When he returned to the den, Mills was right behind him. Trae spoke briefly with him and congratulated him on the birth of his daughter before excusing himself and giving them some privacy.

"Hey," Trish said as she pulled her legs close to her chest.

"I've been calling you. Why did you leave?"

"You needed some time with your daughter. Besides, I needed to get away from there and clear my head," Trish answered honestly. "I already know you think I'm trying to run and that's not it at all, so you can breathe easy."

She may have meant it as a joke, but Mills released the breath that he had literally been holding. He didn't know what to think when he came out to the hospital lounge to find that Trish was no longer there. Immediately after the birth of his daughter the day before, Mills had ordered a DNA test and had them rush it. The hospital had called that morning to inform him that they had his results and he and Trish flew up to the hospital.

Regardless of if he couldn't stand Porsha, he couldn't front and say that he didn't feel an instant connection the moment he held his daughter in his arms. The feeling was unexplainable, but in a good way. It had him wondering why he had waiting so long to have kids of his own. Now he was anxious to see what he and Trish's baby would look like.

"Man, you had me sweating for a minute," Mills said pulling her to her feet and into his arms. "I love you."

186

"I love you, too," Trish said leaning up and kissing his lips. "I would love you even more if you fed me."

Mills playfully mushed her in the head and pushed her away from him. "So, I'm only good for feeding you? You ain't right."

"Well, you're good for other things, too." Trish winked. "Come on. I want Thai."

Mills was glad that she already knew what she wanted to eat because any other day they would waste a good hour trying to decide. Instead of dining in, they decided on takeout, so they could take it back to his place. They were cruising the city without a care in the world, enjoying being in each other's presence. Trish could really see herself getting used to this. She just wished they could have gotten their shit together sooner.

They had approached a stoplight and were waiting for it to change when they were stuck on the driver's side by an oncoming car. They were hit with so much force that it forced the car to skid across the intersection. Dazed, Mills shook his head and tried to focus his strength on getting to Trish. Mills glanced down to find that he was trapped between the crushed metal of the car and the airbags. He could hear her moaning out in pain next to him, but there wasn't anything he could do.

Tires screeching and rapid footsteps could be heard approaching them. Fading in and out of consciousness, Mills tried his best to communicate with Trish but no words left his mouth. The last thing he remembered before everything went black was Trish being snatched from the car. He wasn't concerned with himself. He was just glad that they had gotten to her and his child out safely.

When he finally regained consciousness, the first thing he noticed was the annoying sounds of constant beeping. He opened his eyes and looked around, realizing that he was laid up in a hospital bed. Trae, Ty, and Noc were all present. Trae must had heard him moving around because he lifted his head and looked in Mills' direction. He wasted no time rushing to the hospital bed.

"What the fuck happened? Where is Trish?" Trae no time firing questions at him.

"What do you mean where is she? She should be here. They got her out first," Mills answered.

"Who got her out, because the EMT's said that you were the only one on the scene?" Ty damn near yelled.

"The fuck you mean? They got her out! I watched her get taken out before I blacked the fuck out," Mills yelled, causing the machines he was hooked up to, to go crazy.

"Well, it wasn't the fucking paramedics," Ty bellowed.

"Fuck, fuck, fuuuuuuck!" Trae yelled as he repeatedly punched the wall.

"Man, somebody better tell me what the fuck's going on," Mills said as he began to lose his cool.

A nurse same in to try and check his monitors but ran from the room after he yelled for her to get out and not come back in there.

"Brenda's got her. I know she do. I feel that shit," Trae said pacing the floor. "I'm not letting this shit happen again. I'm not!"

"I'm know somebody better get to explaining this shit," Mills said folding his arms across his chest. "Why the fuck would she take her own daughter?"

Trae blew out a breath and dragged his hands down his face. He hated even reliving this, but he had to get over that. The crew never really questioned the beef Trae and his siblings had with their mother and neither of them volunteered any details. Trae didn't see any point in keeping it a secret any longer, so he figured they might as well know.

He opened up and told them about all of the shit they had to put up with when it came to Brenda. The entire reason behind her being in jail was because she had kidnaped her own kids and was planning on killing them. She wanted them to suffer first. She'd beat them every day that they were held captive. Trish's body couldn't handle the beatings, so she came up with a better form of torture for her. She allowed an eight-year old Trish to be violated in the worst way possible and forced her brothers to watch.

At the time Trae had only been twelve, while Ty was fourteen. They'd been helpless and not able to protect their baby sister from the assault of those grown men. That had been a burden that they had been living with for the last fifteen years and it ate them up. It took years before they could try to put it behind them. Except for Ty. For some reason he was convinced that their uncle Tyrell had been amongst the men responsible for his sister's pain.

His uncle had been the reason that Ty had gone to prison when he was only eighteen and spent eight years of his life behind bars.

Tyrell had gone missing around the time Brenda was sentenced. It's not like Ty could have done much at that time anyway. He was still pretty much a kid. As luck would have it, he'd come across his uncle's whereabouts a few years later and couldn't let the opportunity slip through his fingers. Big Ty had damn near begged him to let him handle it, but this was something Ty felt that he had to do himself. He owed Trish that much.

That attempted homicide charge had him wishing that he had listened to his father and let him handle it. Then maybe they wouldn't be still putting up with his shit now.

"I just need to know what the move is," Mills spoke. "Because that bitch has to die. Her and that nigga."

****

"I'm not going to ask you why because I honestly don't care. Ain't no need for wasting any more unnecessary time," Stacey addressed Don Fernando.

A single bullet to the dome was all it took. No point in drawing the process out. He needed to save his energy for his main target because they had something special in store for him.

"What's up, godfather? Didn't think you would every have to see our faces again, did you?" Stacey asked approaching Santana, who looked to be fading in and out of consciousness.

"No, I'm pretty sure he was looking forward to seeing my face again," Sky said, coming to stand next to her brother.

"Am I supposed to be afraid or something?" Santana spoke through his swollen jaw, thanks to Julio. "The two of you are a joke."

"So much of a joke that you went through all of this trouble just to get to me," Sky taunted.

"Little girl, do you really think you're that important? You weren't really a necessity, just a liability. You're nobody without your brother."

"Well, this nobody's about to enjoy killing your ass." Sky smirked.

It was obvious that he was trying to get a reaction out of her with his words and the disappointment was evident all over his face. Stacey laughed at the look on his face.

"You should work on a better poker face," Stacey suggested with a laugh. "Or maybe not. It's not like it matters anymore."

"Enough of the chit-chat, Stace," Sky said impatiently.

"Don't rush me with your 'ole impatient ass. Gone do what the hell you got to do and remember what the hell I said, Skylar." Stacey frowned. "I'm not about to play with you. Don't be overdoing it and shit."

Stacey looked over at Jonas who was carrying some sort of bag. Jonas sat the bag on a nearby table and begin setting up for Sky. Stacey walked over and looked at all the items he was placing on the table.

"What's all this?" Stacey questioned.

"This all on your crazy ass sister," Julio said shaking his head.

STILL THUGGIN'

"Oh, hell no. Acid? A damn machete? Really? What you need all of this for, Skylar?"

"I'm not about to use all of it, Stacey, so calm down. A girl just likes her options." Sky shrugged.

"I told you she was worse than us," Julio mumbled.

Chapter 18

Trish sat staring at Brenda in disgust. If she could, Trish would jump across the table and drag Brenda all up and through the room they were in. The only thing that stopped her was the gun that sat directly in front of Brenda. Trish was a lot of things, but she wasn't crazy. Under different circumstances Trish might have risked it, but she had her unborn child to think about.

"The way you're sitting over there looking, I would think that you weren't happy to see your mother."

"Bitch, you're no mother of mines," Trish spat.

Those were the first words that had come out of her mouth since they had taken her. She would have still been giving them the silent treatment if Brenda had not just said that stupid shit and referred to herself as a mother.

"I see you still have that nasty ass attitude of yours." Brenda shook her head. "I would have thought that you had that fucked out of you a long time ago."

"Bitch, fuck you with your old washed up pussy having ass. You're pathetic as fuck and a sorry ass excuse for a woman," Trish yelled, hocking up as much spit and she could and spitting it right onto Brenda's face.

Reacting quickly, Brenda grabbed up her gun and slapped Trish across the face with it. "You little disrespectful bitch! I should just kill your ass and get it over with!"

Brenda got up from the table and stormed into the bathroom the clean her face. She was the one supposed to be keeping her composure, but she'd let Trish make her lose her cool. Brenda glanced in the mirror and gave herself a quick pep talk.

"Brenda, don't let that little bitch in there get to you. You already let her and those no-good brothers of hers ruin your life! It's time to make them pay. They're the reason you lost everything! Every fucking thing!"

"Yo," Tyrell called knocking on the bathroom door. "Who the hell are you talking to?"

"Don't worry about it! Just make sure you're watching that bitch in there," Brenda snapped.

Just as she was about to exit the bathroom, she heard Tyrell yell. "How the hell y'all get up in my damn house?"

"Is that really all the fuck you have to say?" she heard someone yell back. "Where that bitch at?"

"She's in the bathroom," Brenda heard Trish say.

"Little bitch," Brenda mumbled under her breath.

MEL G

She had to think fast because she knew they were about to be headed her way. She looked damn at her gun and was thankful that she had thought to bring it with her. So far, she had only heard one voice and was unsure of how many people were present in the house. In that moment, she regretted killing Slim. At least that would have been an extra person on their team. But since they didn't have anyone else, she was going to have to improvise.

Brenda listened as heavy footsteps made their way through the house and in the direction of the bathroom. Determined not to go down without a fight, Brenda raised her gun and aimed it at the bathroom door. Instead of twisting the knob like she had been expecting, the door was kicked in and came flying off the hedges. The door flew in her direction, causing her to stumble back and trip over the toilet.

Ty stepped into the bathroom with a man she didn't recognize standing directly behind him. They both had their guns trained on her. If she didn't know any better, she would say that he probably wanted to kill her more than she knew her children did. He glared at her like he was ready to end her life then and there.

"What's up, mommy dearest?" Ty said and snatched her up by her hair.

Brenda was putting up a good fight, kicking and screaming as Ty dragged her to the front of the house. A boot to the face caused her head to violently jerk back and ceased all movement from her.

"Damn, Noc. Did you snap the bitch's neck?" Trae questioned.

"Man, her ass okay," Ty said waving Trae off. "She shouldn't have been doing all that extra shit. Brenda get your dramatic ass up! Bitch, you ain't dead!"

Ty tossed her across the room as if she weighed nothing. She groaned in pain when her body connected to the hard floor. Trish walked over and drew her leg back, sending a vicious kick to her midsection. She kneeled close so that they could be eye level.

"As much as I want to beat your ass, I'm not about to risk my baby's health. Your pathetic ass ain't worth the energy."

"Fuck you. You're just a weak bitch! Don't try to use that bastard baby as an excuse," Brenda choked out.

Trish reared back and kicked her again, but this time in the mouth. Blood spurted out all over the floor as Brenda yelled out in pain. Trae pulled Trish back as Taz, Laiah, and Kay all walked in. He pulled up a chair and positioned it right in front of where Brenda lay on the floor. Trish took a seat and crossed her legs.

"I may not be the one to beat your ass, but I'm damn about to enjoy the show."

Trish sat and watched as Tyrell and Brenda both were beat to a bloody pulp. By the time the crew was finished with them they were both holding on by a thread. Life could be seen slowly slipping away from them. Trish didn't want anyone but her to have the satisfaction of killing them. She grabbed Trae's gun from his waistband and sent identical shots through both of their hearts. As she watched them take their last breaths, she felt a burden being lifted off of her.

Trish hadn't even realized that she was crying until Trae wiped her eyes and pulled her into his arms. She buried her face in his chest and continued to cry. Finally, she felt free. What her mother and uncle did were something that she carried with her daily and she was glad that she could finally put this behind her.

"Let's get out of here. Your boy in the hospital losing his damn mind right now." Trae laughed as they walked out of the house at the same time the cleanup crew was coming in.

****

"Do you know why he requested you come down here?" Ty asked his brother as they grabbed their luggage and headed to the awaiting limo.

"I have no idea. I just hope this ain't about no bullshit," Trae said.

"I don't think this man flew you all the way down here for no reason. Ain't no telling what this about."

"Just go in here with an open mind, Trae. Don't be flying off the handle," Trish cut in.

"You talking like you know what's up," Trae said looking at her curiously.

Trish shrugged and walked ahead of them. "I'm just saying. Keep an open mind."

The entire ride Trae's mind was all over the place trying to figure out what this could be about. He decided not to stress himself any further and was just going to wait the find out. About half an hour later they were pulling up to those familiar gates and driving down that long ass driveway. Even though he had given himself a pep talk on the whole flight to Miami and the whole ride to the estate, he still didn't think he was ready to face Sky yet.

Their limo came to a stop and Stacey stood outside waiting to greet them. Trish hopped out of the car and hurried into his awaiting arms with a huge smile plastered on her face. She had grown to love Stacey during her brief stay in Miami and had started to develop somewhat of a relationship with him. He had sort of become a brother to her in that short period of time.

"How have you been, mami?" Stacey asked after he released her. "Is that a little bump I see?

"I've been great and yes, it is," Trish answered proudly. "Looks, like you're about to be an uncle pretty soon."

"You're right on the money with that one." Stacey laughed scratching the back of his neck.

He turned his attention to everyone else and extended them a greeting before inviting them all inside. Jonas and Josiah were both in the kitchen stuffing their faces with food that the chef had prepared when they all walked in. Unlike the time before, they were actually welcoming this go round and didn't seem the mind them being there.

Trae was thankful for that because he wasn't in the mood to be going at it with their crazy unstable asses his entire stay in Miami. His life had just calmed down and got back to being somewhat normal.

"Where's Sky?" Trish asked.

That was exactly what Trae wanted to know. He hadn't asked because he didn't want to seem too pressed, but the truth of the matter was that he was. He was anxious to see her. This moment had played itself over and over in his head. This could go one of two ways. She would either be pissed off at Stacey for asking him to come or she would be happy to finally see him after all this time apart. He was hoping that it was the latter.

"She and Julio should be back at any minute now. She has an appointment and the doctor's already on his way," Stacey told them.

"I don't know why you let those two out of the house when you know she has an appointment. They're never on time. Be having us waiting around all damn day for them," Josiah joked.

Stacey laughed because he knew Josiah was right. Julio and Sky always decided to pick the days when they knew they had shit to do, to go out trying to do everything under the sun. It never failed that they would always come back late. Those two probably wouldn't even be on time for their own funerals.

"Y'all might as well make yourselves comfortable and grab something to eat. Ain't no telling when Frick and Frat will be back." Stacey laughed.

They were all gathered around the kitchen eating and laughing when they heard the security system chime, signaling someone's arrival.

"What are y'all cooking?" Sky yelled as she made her way to the kitchen. "And where the hell those bags come from up front?"

She froze as soon as she rounded the corner, causing Julio to accidently bump into her. Luckily, he reacted swiftly and caught her by her arm. Even though she had almost just fallen on her face, she was still too focused on the set of eyes staring back at her. Even with her brother and cousins in the room with her, the look in Trae's eyes had her petrified.

"Oh, shit," Ty mumbled as he got a good look at Sky.

"What is this shit?" Trae asked with so much bass in his voice that it echoed throughout the space.

Sky's voice was stuck in her throat. Even if she could bring herself to talk, she wouldn't know what to say to him. The way that his temple throbbed, and his chest heaved up and down made it very obvious that he was seconds away from exploding.

Sky looked to her brother and the blank expression on his face confirmed for her that he was the one responsible for this shit. She couldn't really blame him though. If she had acted as an adult and just told Trae about the baby all of this could have been avoided.

"Answer me, Skylar," Trae demanded, banging his fists against the table and making her jump.

Ty's eyes immediately went to the triplets. He knew they were good for pulling out those damn guns and right about now they would have a good reason to. Trae looked as though he was ready to kill Sky. It surprised Ty that all three triplets held the same expression Stacey did and hadn't budged.

Evidently, they were already aware of Stacey's reasoning behind calling Trae down there. That still didn't change the fact Ty knew without a doubt that if Trae moved wrong in Sky's direction, they wouldn't hesitate to put a bullet in his ass.

"This has to be a fucking joke, man. Skylar, you're pregnant? Why wasn't I informed of this shit?" Trae snapped. "T, you knew about this shit, didn't you?"

"Trae, I swear to god I didn't know. I suspected it, but I didn't know," Trish told him.

"What's wrong with y'all women?" Mills said shaking his head.

"Give them a minute y'all," Stacey said as he stood.

"Nah, that really ain't the best idea," Ty spoke up.

"The doctor's here," Jonas announced. "He's ready for her appointment."

Trae stood from his seat and headed in Jonas's direction. When Sky still didn't move from her position, he paused midstride and sent her a chilling look.

"Let's go, Skylar."

****

"Twins, man? I'm having twins," Trae said still in shock.

He had been sitting in the same spot since the doctor had left the room. Stacey and Trish had long ago left out and now it was just he and Sky left. Sky sat a good distance away from him and kept quiet. She still didn't know what to say to him and she feared saying the wrong thing would set him off.

"Damn. I'm getting a son *and* a daughter. This shit is surreal," Trae spoke, talking to himself.

He hadn't addressed her not once during the entire appointment. Any questions he had went straight to Dr. Baranov. Even questions that of course only Sky could answer. Like if she had been eating properly or if her body was experiencing any significant changes. It was all very petty if you asked Sky. Since he didn't plan on speaking to her, Sky got up to leave the room so that she could join everyone else.

"Sit down," Trae commanded in a tone that left no room for discussion.

Even with being a Don and an infamous crime boss, she listened to what he said and sat her ass down. He stared at her still not saying a word. His hard glare was making her antsy and she began to fidget in her seat.

"Why, Skylar?"

"I don't know, Trae. I was scared," Sky answered. "I know that's not the answer you want to hear, but it's the truth. I was so scared that you would reject me and my baby that I didn't think. There was just so much going on and then here I come popping up pregnant. That just makes things even more complicated."

"I don't want to hear that. You had more than enough time to tell me. I've missed just about this entire pregnancy."

"I didn't find out until I was damn near four months. But even then, when was I supposed to tell you? When you were packing up and walking out on me? I'd rather you walk out of me, than on me and my babies."

"Is that what you think of me, Skylar? I don't care what we had going on. I would never abandon my seeds," Trae said and dropped his head in his hands. "I'm about to be a fucking father, man."

As much as he still wanted to be upset, the joy of finding out about his unborn children was overshadowing all of that.

"Trae," Sky called out catching his attention. He lifted his head and looked in her direction. "Where do we go from here?"

"I don't know, Skylar." Trae sighed. "I don't know."

Epilogue

"Come on, TJ. You got it, big man. Come to mommy." Sky cheered her son on as he tried to crawl to her.

"Baby, get Taylor. You don't see her lil' ass trying to eat the damn grass?" Trae laughed as he stood over the grill with Noc next to him.

Sky turned around just in time to catch Taylor trying to stuff her chubby cheeks with a fistful of grass. Sky lightly spanked her hands to get her to release the grass, but she was still fighting to get it in her mouth. Taylor fussed and hit back at Sky every time she moved her hand away from her mouth

"Little girl, you're going to make me pop your greedy behind. Put the grass down." Sky laughed.

"You better not pop my damn baby," Trae fussed. "I'm gon' pop your big-headed ass."

"Boy hush. Her lil' bad butt needs to be popped," Trish said as she came and took Baby PJ from his father's arms.

"Why you come over here missing with us? He was chilling?" Mills said sacking her hard on the ass.

"Ow, asshole. Don't be hitting me like that." Trish pouted.

"That's what your ugly ass gets for calling my princess bad," Trae instigated.

"Whatever, nigga. She still a lil' badass," Trish joked. "When Ty and Lay getting here?"

"They should be pulling up in a minute. Said they had to make a stop."

"Okay. Baby, I'm about to go feed PJ and put him down for his nap," Trish said, kissing Mills on the lips. "Baby girl's already knocked out. I'm sure she'll be back up before her mom comes to get her."

"Aight. Cool," Mills told her and took a sip from his beer.

"Aye, tell Bo and Kay their ass better not be fucking in my house," Trae called behind her. "And tell his punk ass to bring the rest of the meat out here."

Trae wiped the sweat from his forehead and closed the grill, before making his way over to his little family. He lowered himself down onto the blanket that Sky had spread out on the grass for the twins to crawl around on.

He scooped up Trae Jr. and tossed him into the air, causing him to release a fit of giggles. Taylor took her focus off the grass long enough to noticed that her daddy had now joined them and made her way to him as fast as she could. Once she was close enough, she pulled herself up onto his legs and tried to push her brother out of the way.

"Don't be trying to take over little girl," Sky said.

"Leave her alone. She can be all over her daddy if she wants to," Trae said grabbing Taylor up in his other arm. "I think mommy's jealous Tay-Tay. Tell her to leave you alone."

"Ain't nobody jealous of her lil' spoiled behind. She needs to stop acting like can't nobody else have your attention and you need to stop spoiling her so much."

"Man, gon' somewhere with that mess." Trae placed both babies back down on the blanket.

Trae moved closer to Sky and kissed the side of her neck. She tried to move away because she was ticklish there and it was her spot. Trae stopped her and pulled her into his lap. He continued nibbling on her neck and moved to whisper in her ear. Sky blushed as he began to vividly describe everything he planned on doing to her body later.

"Aye, cut that shit out! Y'all see my niece and nephew right there," a voice called from behind them.

Sky instantly hopped up at the sound of Stacey's voice and rushed over to where he and her cousins stood. When she was close enough, she jumped into her brother's arms.

"Bubby!"

"Damn, girl. Quit acting like you ain't just see me last month." Stacey chuckled. "If you would have stayed your butt in Miami you wouldn't miss me so much. You done started a family and went into retirement on me."

She playfully punched him in the chest and moved to give her cousins a hug. "Not retirement. More like an intermission."

"What's up, man?" Trae handed Taylor off, who was reaching for her uncle.

"Shit, man. Just living. What's up, Tay? You missed, Unc?" Stacey smothered her with kisses. "Lil' TJ. What's up, playa?"

They all turned to the commotion coming from the house. Ty and Laiah were in what looked to be an argument, while Bo and Kay walked behind them laughing.

"Don't say shit else to me Tyree. I know you did this shit on purpose, so don't even lie," Laiah fussed.

"You damn right I did. I'm a grown ass man. What the hell I got to lie for?"

"I can't stand yo' ugly ass," Laiah said plopping down on the deck chair. "Hey, y'all."

"Damn, what the hell y'all issue is? Don't be coming over here killing our vibe," Trae said messing with Laiah.

"Man, that's her ass. She's trippin'," Ty said, moving to greet everybody.

"What's wrong?" Sky asked concerned.

"She mad because I just made her ass take a pregnancy test and I was right. So now her lil' ugly ass sitting over there in her feelings," Ty fussed.

"Fuck you, Tyree," Laiah snapped.

Trae laughed and shook his head. "Watch your damn mouth around my kids, girl."

"Really?" Sky said hitting him on the arm. "How you gon' tell her to watch her mouth and you sitting here cussing?"

"That don't count. Damn ain't a cuss word. And what I told you about hitting me? Those lil' ass hands hurt."

Sky couldn't do anything but laugh at her husband. He was a straight character. Trish had finally made it back from putting MJ down for a nap and was now snuggled up with Mills on one of the loungers. Sky looked around at her friends and family laughing and having a good time and couldn't help but smile. A year ago, if you would have told her that this is where they would be, she probably would have called you a liar.

Things weren't perfect by any means, which was expected. They had all been through hell and back, but somehow managed to weather the storm and emerged stronger than ever. Regardless of where they were in life, they would always have each other's backs. Some things in life were bound to change, but the bond that they all shared wasn't one of them. One thing that the world could always count on was the fact that they would forever and always be STILL THUGGIN'!

CPSIA information can be obtained
at www.ICGtesting.com
Printed in the USA
LVHW011049150122
708671LV00015B/154

9 781536 846409